SEEING IS BELIEVING

Aelvarim asked, "Do you believe in Fairy yet?"

"I think I'm dreaming." Piper accepted the napkin Malraux extended to her. She wasn't expecting him to pinch her arm, hard. "Ouch."

"You're not dreaming." Malraux offered a napkin to Aelvarim.

"Malraux," Aelvarim scolded. "I brought her here to convince her to help me find Grandmother Dickerson's murderer and save the story, not to be pinched and tormented."

"Got to be the husband or the butler," Malraux said, seating himself beside Aelvarim. "That's traditional."

Aelvarim frowned at him. "Grandmother Dickerson was a widow. And she had no butler."

Piper nodded. "And these days the traditional murderer is a boyfriend or lover."

They both stared at her, eyes wide and jaws slack.

Recovering first, Malraux whispered, "I think she'll do."

ECCENTRIC
CIRCLES

REBECCA LICKISS

ACE BOOKS, NEW YORK

ECCENTRIC CIRCLES

An Ace Book / published by arrangement with the author

PRINTING HISTORY
Ace mass-market edition / July 2001

The Penguin Putnam Inc. World Wide Web site address is www.penguinputnam.com

Check out the ACE Science Fiction & Fantasy newsletter and much more on the Internet at Club PPI!

ISBN: 0-441-00828-3

ACE®
Ace Books are published by The Berkley Publishing Group, a division of Penguin Putnam Inc., 375 Hudson Street, New York, New York 10014.
ACE and the "A" design are trademarks belonging to Penguin Putnam Inc.

PRINTED IN THE UNITED STATES OF AMERICA

10 9 8 7 6 5 4 3 2 1

For Alan,
who has supported me through everything.

And for the Oregon Coast Writer's Workshop,
whose intense writing and sleep deprivation
allowed my imagination to stretch
far enough to encompass anything.

ONE

GRANDMA DICKERSON'S FUNERAL WENT WELL, even though Piper was the only mourner wearing black. A little over thirty close family members stood by listening to the crank of the winch lowering Grandma Dickerson's casket into the cold, sandy earth.

Piper brushed at her eye, wishing for tears. She would miss the old dear, but hadn't been able to cry yet. She wondered if the problem was guilt at not seeing her favorite relative in over six years, or if she was just scared that the instability of her life currently left her unable to face her grief. Both seemed incredibly selfish, and unworthy of her great-grandmother's memory. How much had she moaned and complained that her liberal arts degree and a lousy job market left her unemployed and in debt? Grandma Dickerson was more important than that, so why couldn't she cry?

The cemetery flowed over an artificial hill, providing the deceased with excellent mountain views and a grand city overlook. The winter-dried grass crunched underfoot, and the bare trees swayed gently in the chill wind.

The stark, short, marble blocks sat still and uninviting in orderly rows and columns, without a single statue or ornament in sight.

On the other side of the grave, Uncle Clem stood with head bowed, appearing to stare at his darkest, multicolored, tie-dyed T-shirt, and polyester, earth-tone, bell-bottom pants. Beside him, Aunt Gleda's pink, purple, and green flowered muumuu flapped in the stiff spring-time breeze blowing down from the mountains. Piper looked away from her aunt and uncle, only to see her own parents standing next to her, wearing their almost-new Easter finery. She really didn't want to see her mother's hand-painted straw hat with the long, yellow ribbon flowing in the breeze.

Hamlin, Piper's younger brother, shifted his weight from his right foot to his left foot and tucked his right foot up under his tan duster. Piper hadn't bothered trying to tell him that April in Colorado was not the time for going barefoot. He wouldn't have listened anyway. At least he'd come up from New Mexico for the funeral. He'd worn the duster, completely buttoned, through the entire funeral, viewing and all. It made him look like a flasher who'd stumbled onto a funeral and was waiting for the right opportunity to ruin the proceedings.

After the casket had been lowered, the funeral director glanced from person to person, appearing to be at something of a loss. Piper tried not to come under his notice, but he'd latched on to her quickly as an island of sanity. Someone behind her nudged Piper hard enough to make her step forward.

She glanced back to see Aunt Nellie, her mother's sister, making shooing motions.

From beside the funeral director, Grandma Dickerson's brother, Feargus Ruffcorn—a tall, gray-haired scarecrow of a man—waved her forward. "He wants someone to throw the first handful of dirt onto the grave."

Piper blinked and caught her breath to protest. "She was your sister. You should have that honor."

Great-uncle Feargus patted her shoulder. "You go ahead, dear."

She momentarily considered telling the funeral director that, once someone got them started, there was no telling what this crowd would throw in the grave. But she wasn't in charge of handing out truth today. The sandy dirt trickled easily through her fingers to patter on Grandma Dickerson's casket.

Great-uncle Feargus followed suit with dirt and a few dried wildflowers. Everyone else took turns, adding poems, books, knickknacks, and faux jewels along with the dirt. The funeral director wisely didn't say anything.

As per the instructions Grandma Dickerson had given Great-uncle Feargus, the party retired to Flannagan's for the wake. Jorge directed them into a dark side room, away from the bar. In the side room all the green-tablecloth-covered tables had been pushed together to make two rows, each row surrounded by twenty bent-wood chairs. The room overlooked the parking lot, not that much could be seen through the smoke-tinted square windows.

Even before everyone arrived and was seated, Jorge's staff began setting plates of corned beef and cabbage with mashed potatoes on the tables, and pouring beer and ale into mugs. Jorge tapped Piper's shoulder. "Water?"

"Yes, please." Piper settled the napkin onto her lap and sipped her water.

Hamlin took the seat next to hers, but their parents sat across the room on the other row, next to Uncle Clem and Aunt Gleda. Piper's view of her parents was blocked when her cousin Africa dropped into the chair across from her. Africa pushed her long, curly, honey blond hair back out of her pale blue eyes. Africa had acquired her name by being born in Africa while her parents were in the Peace Corps. "Hi, Lin. Hi, Pi. You doing okay?"

"I'm fine."

Africa's husband, Sherlock Telfour, sat down. A visual contrast to his wife, Sherlock was a very dark-skinned black man. Africa maintained it was love at first sight when he introduced himself in high school with the words, "My name is Sherlock. My father was a big fan of Sherlock Holmes. However, it means blond one." His attention was on Uncle Clem, and the look on his face spoke eloquently of his disquiet. Piper could tell that Africa squeezed Sherlock's hand under the table, for reassurance no doubt.

Sherlock glanced at his wife, then across the table. A look of relief and a hint of a smile crossed his face when his eyes met Piper's. "Hi, Pi. Hi, Lin."

United in a common bond, the dislike of their names, Piper wondered why none of the four of them had ever filed the papers to change it. Piper Pied. She'd always used the excuse of family loyalty to stop herself from changing her last name, but could never find an adequate excuse for not changing her first name. What was it with their parents' generation that made them give those names to their children?

The room had filled with friends and relatives of the deceased, milling about, greeting each other, and gossiping. Great-uncle Feargus tapped his fork against an empty glass for attention. "Since everyone is here, go ahead and start eating. We'll probably do the reading during dessert."

Murmuring voices, laughter, the tinkle of ice against glasses, and the clank of utensils against plates filled the room for a while. The four cousins ate without speaking. At the top of their table, Great-uncle Feargus carried on a heated debate with Aunt Nellie on the overuse of special effects in movies to cover a dearth of plot, characters, and acting. Hamlin rolled his eyes. Piper almost wished for the days when they'd been relegated to a kids' table in another room. She would have bet money Sherlock would have preferred it, too. He hadn't known anything about Africa's family when he was younger, and therefore wouldn't have even been there. Piper always wondered if Africa had hidden her relatives from Sherlock until after he'd said for better or for worse.

They finished eating quickly. Sherlock leaned across the table to whisper, "I'm sorry we couldn't make the funeral."

"That's all right." Piper folded her green napkin. "It was rather windy and brisk. You can always visit the grave later."

Hamlin pushed his plate away. "It's too bad the law wouldn't let Grandma be buried on her own property like she wished."

Great-uncle Feargus tapped his glass again for attention. "As per Alfreida's wishes we'll have the reading of the will first, then anyone who wishes can take a turn telling a humorous anecdote about her or her life. She wanted to encourage all of us to laugh. She didn't want her death to be a sad occasion. Personally, I think if that's what she wanted, she should've made herself a mint to be dished out on her death, but she didn't consult me on that."

He paused for a scattering of laughter. "Alfreida was a good sister and a fun person, and I think we should all do our best to smile when we remember her."

Opening his coat, he pulled a sheaf of papers from the pocket inside. "And now, the moment we've all been waiting for." He settled his glasses better onto his nose, looked at the papers, sorted them, and cleared his throat, before reading. "Says here, Last Will and Testament of

Alfreida Dickerson. Sound mind and all that legal stuff. Etc. Etc. Ah, here we go. The estate is to be settled out and divvied up as follows. All moneys from all accounts, investments, insurance settlements, and such are to be combined and divided into six equal portions. One portion allotted to each of my grandchildren: Gleda Van Kekwik, Tuesday Pied, Nellwyn Fletcher, and Evan Dickerson." He smiled at Aunt Gleda, Piper's mother, Aunt Nellie, and Africa's father, in turn. "My brother, Feargus Ruffcorn, is to receive a double portion." He grinned largely at that, shaking the papers. He took a deep breath and frowned, before continuing. "The house, because of certain preexisting legal agreements, is to be figured separately. The house, with its property and contents, is to be given to whoever throws the first handful of dirt onto my grave."

Piper gasped. He had to have known in advance. Looking around the room, she realized several people knew in advance.

Africa leaned across the table. "Who threw . . . Oh, no. Didn't anyone warn you?"

"No. No one ever warns us," Hamlin drawled.

Great-uncle Feargus smiled at Piper. "We have a few papers for you to sign." He motioned for Aunt Nellie to take over. "You lead the wake for a while. I need to speak to Piper."

Piper walked to a corner of the room with Great-uncle Feargus. The sound of Aunt Nellie talking followed them, but Piper didn't bother distinguishing the words. She took a deep breath to calm herself. "So, what are the preexisting legal arrangements?"

"We wanted you to have the house." He took her shoulders in his gnarled, age-spotted hands and leaned down to kiss her forehead. A little light filtered in through the tinted windows to make his gray hair appear yellowish. "We knew how much you loved books, what with being an unpublished writer and all. They really should be organized and cataloged. It's a very picturesque place. Something right out of a story, really."

Up close his green-and-orange houndstooth check suit made her head ache as much as his words. Picturesque probably should be translated as run-down, and her liberal arts degree hadn't included any library science. She shuddered. "What are the preexisting legal arrangements?"

"You'll be getting a fully stocked house. Furniture, utensils, linens, everything." Great-uncle Feargus's green eyes smiled down on her. "It's a wonderful place for a writer. Perfect for writing. All you'd need is a part-time job, if you kept the garden up and such. Alfreida got by on only social security."

"The legal arrangements?"

"You can't sell it." He ran his gnarled hands through his hair, pushing it into new messiness. "Well, you can sell it, but at a terrible loss. See, when they went to build the suburbs around Alfreida's house, she wouldn't sell. Several of the builders were so persistent that she figured a way to get rid of them. She had legal papers drawn up and signed by herself and the largest builder. Basically the papers say that for twenty-five years from the time of signing the property can't be sold unless it is to that builder, at the price he quoted her first." Great-uncle Feargus sighed. "That was only eight years ago. And the papers are binding on her heirs."

Piper blinked and stared, horrified. "You're telling me I now own property I have to pay taxes and upkeep on, but can't sell for at least seventeen years?"

"That's about it." He grinned. "You're young, seventeen years will pass quickly. You'll see." He patted her shoulder again. "You have to sign some papers, then you can get settled in."

Great-uncle Feargus wandered back to the table and

took control of the wake from Aunt Nellie, who was leading everyone in an Irish drinking song. Piper remained standing in the corner. No job. No money. And now she'd inherited what had to be a money pit.

Somehow, she knew that no objection she could raise would work with her family. The house was hers now, like it or not.

Sitting in her car, in Flannagan's parking lot, Piper looked through the papers Great-uncle Feargus had given her. Certain papers had to be filed with the county or state, others were hers to keep. There was a letter from Grandma Dickerson to whoever inherited the house. On one page of Flannagan's stationery, wheedled from Jorge, Piper's father had scribbled directions. That had been insulting. Piper remembered the way to Grandma's house.

A bit of doubt crept in as she looked at the directions. She hadn't seen Grandma Dickerson in six years; she'd been too busy with college and her life. She hadn't been to Grandma Dickerson's house in longer than that. They'd last seen each other at a Thanksgiving dinner, but Piper hadn't been to Grandma's house in years and years. It was too small to be a family gathering place.

The directions weren't what she remembered of the route to Grandma's house. She decided she'd find the house first, see what she'd need to get before she moved in, then see about getting her stuff moved over from her parents' house.

Through college, and since, Piper had more or less lived a vagabond life, without any fixed address. Her stuff had simply piled up at her parents', in her old room, stored more than used, except for some clothes that went wherever she did. Her clothes were currently in suitcases at her parents' house, a few mountain ridges west, since she was currently between homes.

A knock on the car's window drew Piper's attention

away from the papers. Aunt Nellie peered through the window, waved, and opened the passenger-side door. She held a business card out to Piper. "Something else for you, dear. I talked with Mr. Martin Gumble, he's the manager of Independent Books, he said if you want a job to be there at three P.M. sharp tomorrow, and be prepared to work."

Managing a smile, Piper took the card, and said, "Thank you."

Aunt Nellie waved and left.

Piper sighed and turned the key. "Come on, baby." The engine thought about it, coughed, and turned over. She drove the old, blue Chevy Nova out of the nearly empty parking lot and into the busy traffic on University Boulevard.

Following the directions took her into the northwest end of the city, into a newer suburb of two- and three-car-garage houses, of earth-tone brick and siding, with one staked-straight tree and five generic shrubs in each small green yard. Little children rode bicycles on the sidewalks and streets; older children played basketball with portable hoops in driveways. A jogger in brilliant purple and yellow waved at Piper from the opposite side of the road.

None of it looked as Piper remembered. Her memory supplied a narrow, pothole-filled road that rambled in and out, over hills and across a small stream. The road had been surrounded only by scrub and pine trees. Long ago, Piper had looked out at the tops of the hills to see the city below. Now she could catch occasional glimpses, only if the top of the hill coincided with the space between two houses.

At the end of a long cul-de-sac, Piper spotted a stand of old pines and scrub. A gravel driveway led into them. As she parked the car beside the small house and in front of the detached garage, she estimated that approximately one to two acres of pines and scrub surrounded the house like a fortress, blotting out the suburbs beyond.

In the center of the clearing sat a picturesque, tiny, Victorian gingerbread cottage. The house had always reminded Piper of a face; the two attic gables were eyes over a smiling covered porch mouth, the porch railing made the lower teeth and the gingerbread fretwork above made the upper teeth. The body of the house was the same pale pink it had always been, and brown shingles still covered the roof. But the white accents had changed. The rails and decorations were now painted in the vibrant colors of the rainbow.

It reminded her so powerfully of her great-grandmother that she had to catch her breath. Piper climbed the stairs to the front porch. Everything reminded her of her great-grandmother. Using the key, she opened the door. Inside the parlor, the familiar smell of books, old dust, mothballs, and lavender overcame her. She expected to see Grandma Dickerson walk through the door to the kitchen any moment. Tears streamed down her face. She stood in the doorway, crying, finally. After a while she composed herself, so that she could see to navigate the room.

Bookshelves lined all four walls. A window seat stacked high with newspapers and magazines protected the heavy gold brocade curtains at the front window. In the center of the room a low, small table nearly bowed under the weight of books on it. Three Queen Anne chairs surrounded it, holding their own stacks of papers. A conversational sat in the front corner of the room, covered in cloth-bound journals. A fainting couch rested under the side window, amazingly clear of anything but dust.

Piper negotiated her way through the chairs and table to the kitchen door. On her right in the kitchen a small corner housed the cupboards and stove. A sink and refrigerator held up the wall along the side of the house. A table with two chairs guarded the back door of the house. Books and papers covered all flat surfaces, and small bookshelves were placed throughout the room.

On her left was the door to the bathroom, which if Piper remembered rightly, had been half tucked under the stairs to the attic, making standing up from the toilet something to be done with caution. A glance confirmed her memory. A small, filled magazine rack clung to the wall by the toilet.

Next to the bathroom door was the bedroom door. Filled bookshelves on all four walls surrounded a floral canopied bed. Narrow walkways surrounded the bed and led to a small wardrobe tucked into the far corner. The window seat under the front window was clear but dust-covered, and Piper pushed the floral curtains back to allow some light into the room. She did the same with the curtains on the side window.

The yellow-and-red rose-patterned bedspread had no dust on it. The lace and frills on the pillows were starched and stiff. Someone had changed the sheets and tried to fix up a little for her. Piper suspected Aunt Nellie. Grandma Dickerson had died in the hospital, so Piper didn't have to worry over any residual ickiness about sleeping in the bed.

Piper ignored the door leading to the attic stairs. She'd look up there later. She tossed her purse on the bed, and the papers and Grandma's letter spilled out onto the bedspread. Sitting on the bed, Piper picked up the envelope. Opening it, she found a single sheet of lined yellow paper and read the faint scrawled script.

"To the new owner of my house: I know it's small and may seem cramped, but if you'll give it time, you'll find a wonderland within its walls. The books have served me well, better than most people. There are hidden treasures in them, if you know how to look. Some of the neighbors may seem strange, and some of them truly are, but if you give them a chance, you may find they, too, are a pleasant surprise. Don't form a hasty opinion, Dearest, of the house or of the people. Remember not to judge a book by its cover. I hope and pray you are as happy here as I was. Love, Alfreida Dickerson."

After another good cry, Piper put the letter back in the envelope. It was good to know Grandma had been happy here. Piper wiped the last of the tears from her eyes. She tried to pull herself together; there was work to be done.

With a deep breath, she stood up, and headed out of the room, trying to figure out what she'd need to get to settle into the house. She started by looking into the kitchen cupboards, to see what she had.

A few old cans and boxes of food huddled in the upper cupboards. Piper figured she was probably only slightly better off than Mother Hubbard. In the lower cabinets, some old leaking cleaner bottles hid behind a fortress of books and magazines. She decided she'd be better off trashing everything in the cupboards and starting fresh.

Searching the countertops, she found a blank scrap of paper and a pencil, and started a list. Dust rags headed the list. Followed by food and cleaners. She wandered through the house, trying to think of what she'd need. By the time she finished her list, ending with toilet paper, the sun had started to set.

She drove carefully through the suburbs in the growing dim, trying to find landmarks in the sameness, so she could find her way back in the dark. It was near midnight when she made the return trip, with only her clothes and a few things from her list gathered at her parents' house.

The sun, streaming in through the windows, woke

Piper in the morning. She snuggled deeper into the softness of the bed's old mattress, feeling the crispness of the starched sheets. After alternating a few moments between stretching and snuggling, she swung her legs out from under the sheets and set her bare feet on the cool wooden floor. She kept her eyes half-closed, the better not to see the dust and mess, and wandered into the kitchen.

She leaned on the counter by the stove, rubbing her eyes until she could focus on the scraps of paper with recipes scribbled on them. As she opened the cupboard door to look to see what she'd brought to eat for breakfast, the feeling that something was different gripped her. The tangled mess of recipes looked the same. The stove, the refrigerator, and the sink looked the same. The kitchen table was still covered with papers and junk.

But the handsome, dark-haired, blue-eyed man sitting at the table hadn't been there last night.

TWO

THE MAN STARED AT PIPER IN WIDE-EYED surprise. She hoped she didn't also look like some deer trapped by an oncoming car's headlights. She was acutely aware of the short, satiny, spaghetti-strap chemise nightshirt she had on. She wished she'd worn her heavy flannel granny gown. She tried to clear her mind, and think where in the kitchen Grandma Dickerson might have kept her butcher knives.

"Who are you? What do you want?" Piper inched along the counter, hoping to make it to the other side of the room, and the phone.

"I beg your pardon," he said. He stood and bowed to her, sweeping his blue, calf-length cape behind him. "I am Aelvarim. Forgive me, but you startled me."

Now that he was standing, Piper could see that he wore some sort of old-fashioned tunic, light tan in color, which appeared to be made out of some sort of hide. Possibly his own, it was that tight across his chest and shoulders. His legs were encased in hose or leggings, apparently painted on, in a blue color that exactly matched his cape. Tan pointed boots completed his ensemble. No, she'd missed the blue feathered hat on the table.

"I startled you?" Piper gulped her fear down. She'd made it to the sink, and he'd made no move toward her. Another quarter of the room, and she'd grab the phone. "This is my house. What are you doing here?" She didn't like his intense stare; it made her nervous.

Aelvarim reseated himself, and began to hum.

Piper relaxed. She couldn't think of any reason why she was suddenly less nervous, but now that her shaky legs could actually carry her to the phone, she was loath to go. She took a deep breath and walked to the phone.

"I would never hurt you," he said quietly, before he resumed humming.

Her hand touched the phone, but she couldn't look away from him. He'd certainly had a more-than-adequate chance to attack her, but he just sat there looking . . . cute. His large blue eyes expressed only innocence. He hadn't even leered at her, for pity's sake, and there she was with nearly nothing on. It was almost insulting.

For the first time she saw the red sheen of his hair, and realized that it wasn't black, but a very, very dark red. His face seemed almost to glow a deep golden. Her gaze traveled down his face from his bright, blue eyes, past his full lips and smooth chin, down his golden neck, to where the ties of his tunic had carelessly come undone and opened, revealing a small portion of his golden chest. She watched his chest rise and fall as he breathed, and fancied she could see the slight bump of each beat of his heart, barely hidden under the thin, taut hide of his tunic.

He stopped humming, and Piper realized she was sitting across the kitchen table from him. "You have my name, may I know yours?"

"Piper Pied," she said absently as she started to stand.

Aelvarim's face lit in a wide smile. "Oh, you're Grandmother Dickerson's great-granddaughter. She told me much about you. Please, may we talk?"

Piper sat back down. He had to be one of Grandma's flaky friends. Could he be one of the neighbors Grandma had mentioned in her letter? She couldn't imagine him living nearby and Grandma not attempting some sort of matchmaking with great-granddaughters, or other young single female relatives. Still, she'd have to discourage him from just walking in and making himself to home. Though, there were worse sights to see first thing in the morning.

"I wanted to talk with whoever inherited the house about Grandmother Dickerson's murder." He stared at her seriously and intently. "We have to find the murderer and finish the story, or everything we know will be destroyed."

He was cute; even though he dressed like a refugee from a renaissance fair and had a dramatic flair for finding murder and ruin in everyday life. Piper sighed. "Grandmother Dickerson died of complications of old age, stroke and heart failure. The doctors said so."

"No, she was murdered." Staring intently, Aelvarim leaned toward her. "Whoever did it knew well the use of magic. For they twisted the arcane arts to accomplish their hideous deed, and mask it in the guise of the ordinary."

"Magic." Piper tried not to smile. How could he be so sincere and so mistaken at the same time? "I suppose you know all about magic."

Sighing, Aelvarim slumped in his chair shaking his head. His hair fell in thick locks around his face. "No. I'm not accomplished in the recondite arts. I am but a novice. I can do a few tricks only." He pulled himself up. "Still, I will not leave Grandmother Dickerson's murder unavenged." He pushed his hair back from his face.

His long, tapering, elegant fingers caught Piper's attention as they slid through his smooth, shiny, dark red hair, combing it away from his face. It was only as his fingers brushed against his ears that she noticed the tall, golden points of his ears sticking out of the dark locks.

"I know the murderer was of Fairy, because I can feel the rift between the worlds of Fairy and Human. I'm a storysmith."

"The murderer was a fairy?" Piper tried to examine his ears surreptitiously. She couldn't see any demarking line between his flesh and the false points.

"That's possible, I suppose, but I can't see any of them putting themselves to that much effort. No, I suspect it is someone else. I can feel the change in the story, as if someone has tried to warp it to their ends."

Piper gave up searching his ears and decided to be blunt. "And, you're a fairy, too?"

She'd never seen anyone look so indignantly wounded before. Obviously piqued, Aelvarim fussed with the shoulders of his cape.

"No. I'm an elf. Not a fairy, an elf. Aelvarim means 'victorious army of elves.' I was named after . . . Never mind. The important thing is, I'm an elf."

Realizing she'd touched on a sore spot, Piper quickly said, "I'm sorry. I didn't mean to offend." Suddenly she remembered that this was her house, and he was the intruder. "Look, what are you doing here, and what do you want? Get to the point."

He returned to staring intently at her. "I need you to help me find the murderer and fix the story. If we can complete the story, we can heal the rift that's tearing our worlds apart from each other, and everything will continue as it should."

Piper couldn't help smiling. "And they lived happily ever after. The end."

"If it were only that easy." Aelvarim shook his head. "Grandmother Dickerson's house, because of the mass of stories here and Grandmother Dickerson herself, has become a connecting point between the world of Fairy and the world of humans. But, I'm afraid Grandmother Dickerson's knowledge and power brought her to the attention of someone with a very evil mind." He leaned across the table, scattering paper and books, to whisper, "She was writing a story, you know. I think that she knew what was happening, and put clues into her manuscript, in case anything happened. Which, unfortunately, it did."

Automatically catching the books before they could fall, Piper restacked the piles on the table. "Look, Aelvarim, I'm sure you believe everything you're saying. And, undoubtedly, it would be fun to search the house for treasure, or another will, or an unpublished manuscript, but maybe another time. I need to get breakfast, and get dressed, and I might actually have a job to go to, so why don't we let it go for now? We'll look into it later. Sometime." Piper stood, went to the back door, and opened it. Hoping he'd get the hint and leave. Also, it put her closer to the phone if he chose not to take the hint.

Aelvarim looked pained. He leaned back in the chair, stretching out his long, long legs, and hummed. She noticed his legs crossed at the ankles, just at the top of his boots. His legs were lean and muscular, without being thick, and the tights clung nicely to his legs while displaying every inch.

When he stopped humming, Piper realized she was sitting at the kitchen table again.

"There truly is a world of Fairy," Aelvarim said quietly. "And some power from it did murder your great-grandmother. And I need your help, as the new owner of this house connecting the two worlds, to find the murderer and fix the story."

"Yes, I write, but I'm not published." Piper found herself getting angry along with defensive. Now not only did she have this mess to sort through in the house, but this idiot wanted her to rewrite Grandma's manuscript. If such a thing existed. "I'm not sure what's wrong with my own writing. I don't think I could fix anyone else's manuscript."

"No, I didn't mean Grandmother Dickerson's manuscript." Aelvarim sat up straight. "I meant your grandmother's life, this house, Fairy, and Human. The things that are happening here, what is going on."

"Life," Piper said. "Life is what is happening here. My great-grandmother died, and life is going on. Life is not a story."

"Depends on your perspective, doesn't it."

Maybe if she fed him, he'd go away. He was certainly cute, and very nice to look at, but she had serious concerns about his sanity. Not that he appeared to be dangerous, he just acted like he didn't live in the same world with everyone else.

"It's too early for this." Piper stood up. "I'm going to get dressed, then I'll fix breakfast, and we can talk."

His eyes flicked down, then up, as he looked her over. "You appear to be dressed now."

Piper walked to the bedroom and shut the door behind her without a word. It had no lock. That worried her, but she reminded herself that it also meant there was no keyhole in the door. She walked through the cluttered room, closing the window curtains. From the suitcase balanced precariously on several stacks of books, Piper pulled clothes, choosing jeans and a large, floppy sweater to wear.

Back in the kitchen, she found Aelvarim still seated

at the table. He smiled uncomfortably at her as she rummaged around, pulling out bread for toast and eggs to scramble. She turned to face him. "So, did you want some breakfast, too?"

He hesitated, glancing from the items she'd pulled out, to her face, to the back door, and back to her face. "I suppose it wouldn't hurt anything." She'd started the eggs when he asked, "Could I be of some assistance? Or would you prefer I stayed out of your way?"

"Sure, you can make the toast." Piper tossed him the loaf of bread, and watched as he examined the clear plastic wrap and twist tie.

"Toast," he said uncertainly, looking around the room. He'd discovered the secret to the twist tie, and was slowly unraveling it. "Where is your fire?"

"Just make them in the toaster." She brushed aside the recipes and pulled the faded, quilted, hen cover from the shiny metal toaster.

Piper couldn't help smiling as he looked the toaster over thoroughly, then reexamined the bread. He certainly took his insanity seriously. She managed to stir the eggs, and keep an eye on him. He gingerly put a slice of bread in each of the two slots, then stepped back, as if expecting it to explode or the bread to shoot out at him.

After a moment Aelvarim stepped forward again, and tensed, as if ready to jump back if he were mistaken. Finally, he relaxed and watched the bread sit in the slots, for developments.

"Push the handle down." She had to turn back to stir the eggs, or she'd have burst out laughing.

Risking a glance over her shoulder, Piper saw Aelvarim pick up the toaster and discover the handle. He set the toaster back down before pushing the handle. As a precaution he stood as far away as he could.

Piper dished up eggs onto two plates, and turned to

Aelvarim as the toast popped up. Holding the plates out, she said, "One on each plate."

He reached for them, and quickly pulled his hand back. "They're hot."

"Yes, they're toasted."

Swiftly, he put one slice on each plate. She set the plates on the table and motioned for him to sit. Piper started another round of toast, grabbed two forks, a knife, margarine, and filled two glasses with water. "Sorry, I don't have any coffee. I don't have much of anything yet."

Aelvarim nodded, while staring at his plate. She started eating, and he watched her for a moment, before tentatively picking up his fork.

"So, you're from Fairy, but you're not a fairy. What are fairies then?" she asked conversationally.

He dropped his fork, and began gesturing with his hands. He held them about six to eight inches apart, to indicate height. "They're about this high. Wings. Nonsensical temperaments and nasty little minds." His hands moved as if twisting or strangling something. "They're everywhere, and constantly stirring up trouble. They're vermin." He stopped himself, as if surprised at his words. He picked up his fork and made an effort to adopt a semblance of serenity. "They're quite different from elves, but they, too, have their place in the scheme of things."

"I see." Piper looked down at the paper beside her plate. It was a list of book titles in Grandma Dickerson's handwriting. "And you think Grandma Dickerson was murdered?"

With a bite of eggs in his mouth, he could only nod. Once having taken the first bite, Piper noticed he ate quickly. She wondered if he'd been expecting to be poisoned. She finished off her eggs and toast. "I don't suppose you'd believe me if I swore that the doctors were sure it was just old age."

He shook his head. Before his next bite, he said, "Murder."

Piper sighed. He was very cute, but she knew she had to return him to his keepers. Undoubtedly they were worried about him being gone from the asylum for so long. And now that she was an adult, with a house of her own and everything, she knew she couldn't give in to the "but I promise I'll take care of him, and feed him, and clean up after him" thoughts. She couldn't afford pets right now.

"Well." Piper tossed her plate and fork in the sink, so as not to be looking at him when she said, "How about you show me where you live, and we can talk some more about this." *We'll talk with your keepers about your delusions, and why you shouldn't be allowed to roam unsupervised.*

She wondered if she'd made a mistake, when he stepped up beside her to put his plate and fork in the sink. He was nearly beaming with joy.

"I'd be honored to show you my home."

THREE

AELVARIM STOPPED HER JUST AS THEY REACHED
the back door. He spoke very seriously. "The doors to
this house can open on either world. Whenever you
leave you must think of the world you want to enter.
It's very important. You must remember."

"I'll remember," Piper assured him breezily. "I promise."

He opened the door and stepped out into the yard,
holding the door gallantly for her. The backyard looked
almost as Piper remembered it. The winter brown lawn
showed much neglect, with the overgrown and broken,
brittle brown grass dotted with dried weeds. The rosebushes by the house looked like bare brown sticks; only
by looking closely could you see the buds that would
develop into leaves beginning to turn green. A flagstone
path wound through the yard past the old, unpainted,
leaning, graying wooden gazebo. The surrounding
pines—impressive Colorado blue spruce, tall and green
and vibrant, with heavy lower branches sweeping the
ground like old-fashioned hoop skirts—blocked any
view of the suburbs around them.

The brilliant Colorado sunshine was missing. Piper looked up. The sky appeared to be a darker blue, with light gray clouds floating through it. She shrugged off an ambiguous feeling of something gone awry. It was springtime in the Rockies; April was a wet, cold, snowy, icy month. The sun didn't shine every day.

Aelvarim started walking down the flagstone path. Piper watched him walk away, realizing for the first time that he carried a quiver slung across his back, over his cape. That explained why the cape covered only one shoulder. She could see several arrows sticking out, and something else. She couldn't tell what it was. A small harp hung from his belt, bouncing off his hip as he walked. The Complete Renaissance Man. Piper couldn't help smiling.

He looked back when he reached the gazebo and motioned her to follow. Once she started, he resumed walking. She stopped at the gazebo. He'd left the flagstone path, which ended at Grandma's empty vegetable garden, and reached the edge of the trees. He stood, smiling, waiting for her.

How crazy was he? Was he luring her to her death? In the forest? Piper almost laughed at herself. There was no forest left here. The suburbs had taken over. On the other side of those trees were three-bedroom, two-car-garage, middle-management dream houses. She joined him and plunged into the shadows between the trees.

The majestic blue spruces gave way to scrawnier, scragglier pines, whose branches weren't as weighted with leaves. The rough pine bark showed through their horizontal branches. The ground was littered with discarded pine needles, making little trails through the trees.

When they hadn't emerged into someone's backyard or the end of a cul-de-sac after a few minutes, Piper's uneasiness grew. Suppose Grandma's house backed not onto another part of the suburb, but onto some still-undeveloped land, or park or something. No, that couldn't be right. She'd seen a map at her parents' house; the suburb surrounded Grandma's house. Even so, the trees should have thinned or given over to open space.

It was awfully warm. Even without her coat, which she usually wore this time of year, she was beginning to overheat in her sweater. The air felt wetter than normal, as if it were raining. She stopped and looked around, unsure of her ability to find her way home.

"This way. Not much farther," Aelvarim said, glancing back as he headed down the rise they had been climbing.

Come into my parlor . . . She was surely condemned now. Fleeing didn't appear to be an option. Piper couldn't tell which way they'd come, or even which direction was which. She couldn't see the mountains through the trees. Perhaps he was a gallant, even chivalrous sort of crazy. Until his other personality came out.

Piper shivered, but followed.

The pines finally thinned. A rolling meadow spread out beyond them. The brilliant green grass was just on the verge of needing a good mow, and a burbling brook meandered through on the left-hand side. It seemed remarkably green for the time of year and altitude, almost picturesquely pastoral. Except for the lack of fluffy white sheep dotting the hills, and the presence of the large stone tower rising at the center.

"I don't think we're in Kansas anymore," Piper quoted, looking nervously at the meadow.

Aelvarim looked at her curiously. "Kansas? I thought Grandmother Dickerson's house was in Colorado."

"Figure of speech." She stared out at the tower. Made of square gray-and-brown blocks, with a crenellated top, arrow slits for windows, and metal-bound wooden door, it appeared to be a perfect storybook tower. Home, possibly, for some wicked witch or imprisoned maiden. "This is your home?"

"Oh, no. This is Larkingtower's spire." Aelvarim stroked the strings of his harp, apparently lost in thought for a moment. "He's . . ."

"What have you done now?" a querulous voice shouted. The wooden door opened outward, to hit against the stone with a resounding crack. A tall, wizened old man, with snow-white hair and flowing beard, stalked out to them. He carried a long staff, seeming to hold it more as a prop than to use it. He wore what appeared to be three layers of long ground-sweeping robes, all but the last cinched at his waist with a length of rope. A tall, dark, pointed hat decorated with glitter rode on his head.

"The wizard, Larkingtower," Aelvarim said, motioning to the old man with his hand. "This is Piper Pied, Grandmother Dickerson's great-granddaughter. She inherited Grandmother Dickerson's house."

Planting his staff firmly into the ground, Larkingtower peered down at her in obvious disgust. "A woman? She left her house to a woman?" He suddenly leaned down to squint at her, his knobby nose nearly touching hers. He straightened up and stepped back, nearly jumping away from her. Pointing a crooked, arthritic finger at her, he accused, "She's a mortal."

"Yes, sir," Aelvarim said blandly. "I went to speak to her about Grandmother Dickerson's murder. She didn't seem to believe in Fairy, so I thought I'd show her."

"You brought her here deliberately!" Larkingtower turned his wrath on Aelvarim. "You brought a mortal into this realm to prove a point?"

"As you see." Aelvarim didn't appear the least alarmed at the fact that smoke was curling off of Larkingtower's staff and out through the folds of his robes.

"I need her help to track down the murderer, complete the story, and heal the rift."

"Fool!" Larkingtower waved his arms out wide, nearly striking Piper with his staff. "She will vex your every waking moment and torment your sleep. She will cloud your vision until you could never find the murderer. She is patently incapable of completing any story. This will not heal the rift." The smoke thickened and enveloped him. When it dissipated, Larkingtower was gone.

"I've finished every story I've ever started," Piper said.

"That went better than I expected." Aelvarim sighed, and smiled down on her. "Of course you finish what you start. I'm certain I can rely on you."

"What's with him?" she asked, motioning to the tower.

"Oh, just his magic tomes, some candles, and other arcane paraphernalia cluttering up the place, his personal effects." Aelvarim looked at the tower and shook his head. "There's really not that much to his spire. I think he prefers it that way. He seems to stick mostly to his magic. I'm not sure he has any other interests."

Piper decided not to attempt the question again, realizing it was better just to move on. "Who is he to you?"

"A mentor mostly. Someone older and wiser I can take my questions to. He's really not so bad, once you get to know him." Aelvarim pointed to a little hillock on the other side of the brook. "Our path is over there."

Following close behind him, Piper wondered about her sanity. Hallucination, perhaps? Had he slipped something into her breakfast? Maybe she'd only dreamed she woke up, and this was all a dream. Yes, that had to be it. She eyed his long dark red hair, curling on his broad shoulders. As dreams went, this was not bad, not bad at all, except that his cape hid the rest of him as he walked in front of her.

He led her to a quaint little arched wooden bridge over the burbling brook. It seemed rather pointless, stretching over an area more than four times the width of the brook. Piper figured she could have jumped over the brook without even a running start.

"The first bridge." He turned around to face her, walking backwards a few steps. "We call it the three bridges path."

"We?" Piper asked.

"Larkingtower, Malraux, and I." He passed over the bridge in three clomping steps. Piper followed quietly. He glanced back over his shoulder at her. "Be careful, there's usually fairies by the streams."

No sooner had he turned around than something whizzed past her nose. It buzzed like a fly, circling her head. It flew in front of her, hovering at eye level, just beyond her reach. It looked like a miniature man, dressed in strange green clothing, with gossamer—almost insectoid—wings. The little man winked at her, holding a finger to his lips.

He flew down, to catch a corner of Aelvarim's cape. Lightning fast, he flew up, bringing the corner of the cape with him, to pull it over Aelvarim's head.

Aelvarim swiftly grabbed the harp at his hip, before lifting the cape from his head. He turned in a circle, looking for his tormentor. "Who is it?"

"I don't know," Piper said, shrugging her shoulders.

He looked at her, as if just remembering her presence. His cheeks colored. "Actually I was asking him. But, what did he look like?"

"About like you described." Piper held her hands about six inches apart. "Green clothes. See-through wings, like a bee's."

"What color was his hair?"

Piper frowned, trying to remember. "Brown, I think."

"Figwort," he said with an authoritative air.

The miniature flying man appeared again, buzzing around Aelvarim's head. He laughed, a surprisingly low-pitched laugh. "Aelvarim, come to sing for us?"

"No," Aelvarim said quellingly. Motioning for Piper to hurry, he turned and began walking away.

The fairy flew to stand on Aelvarim's quiver, grabbed two thick locks of Aelvarim's hair, and yanked back on them, shouting, "Whoa!"

Aelvarim stopped. Piper couldn't see his face, but his voice was thick with false patience when he said, "Let go of my hair."

Four more fairies joined Figwort, flying around an irritated Aelvarim. A miniature woman, with large blue butterfly wings and a matching blue gossamer dress, flew back to examine Piper. She flitted in circles around Piper, stopping to examine and tug at Piper's trouser leg, hand, sweater hem, and neckline. She made a final sweep through Piper's hair, to examine Piper's right ear. She flew back to Aelvarim, inquiring sweetly, "Aren't you going to introduce us to your new lady friend?"

Batting at the other fairies, who were swooping down to pull his hair, Aelvarim just muttered something Piper couldn't hear. The fairies darted away from him as if pushed. Laughing, in what sounded to Piper to be a perfect chord, the fairies soared up into the sky, only to dart back down around her.

"What's your name?" the blue-winged fairy asked.

Piper held her hand out, palm down, for the fairy to land on. "Piper Pied. You have very beautiful wings. What's your name."

The little woman preened and fluffed out her wings. "Meadowsweet." She sailed off, dragging another of the laughing fairies back, to present to Piper. "This is

Horsemint." Another. "This is Bearberry." Another. "Pasqueflower." The last. "Figwort."

"I believe we've met," Piper said, winking at Figwort.

Aelvarim cleared his throat. "We have to be going now. We must see Malraux." He walked off.

Smiling, Piper shrugged and followed him.

Figwort swooped down in front of Aelvarim. "Where did you find the pretty lady?"

When Aelvarim ignored him, Figwort fetched the other fairies. All five dived to catch the hem of Aelvarim's cape. They flew up and around Aelvarim, dragging the cape not over his head this time, but around his neck, so that it hung in front, rather than behind him. Aelvarim choked and reached for his neck.

Perforce pausing, Aelvarim muttered something again, causing the fairies to dart away from him. He pulled the quiver off, over his head, and began turning his cape around. Piper noticed that his left hand remained clutching the harp on his hip.

She tried to step forward to help him, but she couldn't lift her feet from the ground. Looking down she found some sort of creeper vine entwined around her ankles. The vine waved its tiny white flowers as it wrapped itself tighter.

"Ack!" Piper reached down, but the vine attempted to catch her hand in its coils. She heard the perfectly pitched fairy laughter, and straightened up.

"Need help?" Horsemint asked.

"I suppose," she said. The unreality of the situation prevented her from fearing any real problems, and Piper ended up smiling. Aelvarim had finished putting his cape and quiver back. Horsemint flitted to him. "She needs help. Kiss her, and we'll let her go."

Aelvarim recoiled, in dismay.

In an attempt to aid him, Piper said, "Now that's not fair. He shouldn't have to pay my penalty."

Horsemint's flight back to Piper was interrupted by Meadowsweet, who caught hold of Horsemint's feet, to swing him around. "I want a lock of her hair."

Pasqueflower took exception to this, and soon all five fairies were engaged in an aerial dogfight.

Aelvarim approached Piper, but not so close that he'd get entangled in the vine. "If she gets a lock of your hair, she might use it to entangle you in a spell."

"So, if she doesn't get a lock of my hair, she can't entangle me in a spell?" Piper asked.

"Well, no. She still could."

"So what's the difference? What else could she do with it?"

He ducked to avoid a swooping fairy. "She could do anything with it: weave a floor mat, braid a rope, make a spell. Though, the way you put it, I suppose it doesn't make any difference." He pulled a knife from his boot and handed it to her hilt first.

Piper cut a small lock of plain brown hair from close to the nape of her neck, handed the knife back to Aelvarim, and held the lock of hair up in the air.

Meadowsweet flew past, snatching the lock of hair, and Piper felt her ankles freed. Aelvarim took off running into a forest beyond the meadow, with Piper at his heels.

He slowed only after they'd put several rises between them and the fairies. "Nasty vermin."

"They're not so bad," Piper said. She noticed he'd finally let go of his harp.

Aelvarim led her to another brook, this one larger than the first, with a solid, moss-covered, stone bridge. On the other side was a small rock-strewn glade, surrounded thickly by forest, with tree stumps dotting the glade. It almost seemed to Piper as if the brown rocks and weatherworn tree stumps were stationed about as seats. A thick layer of moss and tree leaves carpeted the floor of the glade. At the opposite side, the path continued up a green, grass and tree-covered, hill. A large black arch cut into the side of the hill.

The fanciful carvings on the rock of the cavern entrance made what might have been a forbidding maw into a welcoming inlet. Somehow Piper couldn't be afraid of a place with carved baby birds at the opening. Aelvarim ducked down to enter the cavern. Piper paused to examine one of the carvings, a very cute baby robin with half-closed sleepy eyes, then hunched over and stepped in.

Unable to see, and not brave enough to stand up in case she might hit her head, she stretched her hand out and smacked into a face at about the level of her waist. "I'm sorry."

"Quite all right," an unfamiliar male voice said. A small hand caught hers. "Your eyes will adjust in a moment. If you'll follow me, there's more light farther in."

The size of the hand didn't fit with the adult voice, but the hand itself was heavily callused and rough. The voice was smooth, cultured, intelligent, and lightly accented, though Piper couldn't place the accent. He guided her through the descending tunnel, and helped her negotiate two almost-180-degree turns; after the first turn the light increased. The second was the entrance to a cavern chamber, larger than a normal room, with a high ceiling.

Someone had worked to make it into a home. Most of the light came from a large fireplace, carved into the side of the left-hand wall, by which Aelvarim was standing. A kettle hung from a hook over the fire. Rag throw rugs were scattered here and there. A rough wooden table stood near the fireplace, flanked by two benches. The rest of the furniture appeared to be carved from the stone of the cavern. Stalagmites had been made into chairs and table, a whole conversation pit. Along the opposite wall from the entrance a small cubby in the wall had been converted into a bed. Another tunnel opened on the right-hand wall.

Piper looked down and discovered a small, grubby, long-bearded man holding her hand. He wore a sort of durable, dark-colored tunic and pants, with a stout leather apron. A pair of small leather gauntlets peeked out of the apron pocket.

"Piper Pied, meet Malraux. She is Grandmother Dickerson's great-granddaughter."

"Enchanted," Malraux murmured as he kissed her hand.

"The same," Piper said. She looked at Aelvarim. "That's certainly a better reception than the last."

Malraux barked, "Ha. So you've met Larkingtower." He headed for the fireplace. "Don't let him bother you. He hates everybody. Especially women." He stirred the kettle. "I know it's a little early, but lunch is nearly ready. Would you like some stew?"

She looked over his shoulder into the kettle; the contents looked like stew and smelled wonderfully rich. She glanced at Aelvarim. Aelvarim nodded silently. Malraux didn't miss the exchange, but merely cocked an eyebrow at her. She managed a smile. "Sure."

"Ha." Malraux slipped over to the cubby in the far wall, removing his apron and hanging it on a peg beside the cubby. "Aelvarim, why don't you go outside and conjure up some flowers, while we do something useful, like get lunch on."

"I made toast this morning for her," Aelvarim said in a wounded tone. He pulled himself up as tall as he could.

"Without burning it?" Malraux plunged his hands into a cut-off stalagmite. Water slopped out as he washed his hands.

"She has a toaster," Aelvarim said.

"And that keeps you from burning the toast?" Malraux

leaned over the stalagmite to splash and scrub his face.

"Not always," Piper said. Aelvarim glanced gratefully at her.

Malraux smiled. "Just go get some flowers. We need to brighten up the place for your guest." Aelvarim hesitated a moment and left. Malraux pulled a clean, white, cloth apron from another hook and put it on. "Don't ever ask him to sing. You'll only embarrass him. And don't mention high elves. Or dark elves." He joined her at the fireplace. "He's a fine young elf, but he's very sensitive about certain subjects. Fetch me three bowls." He pointed to a low shelf with a variety of plates, bowls, and platters.

"He can't sing, hmm?" Piper picked up three bowls. "Why high elves or dark elves?"

"His mother's high elven, from over the water. His father's dark elven. Native, more or less, to here. She came back with him after the last great war." Malraux ladled stew into the bowls she held for him. "Aelvarim wants to be high elven, but he's not blond, not a bard, and not from over the waters." Malraux looked up at Piper to catch her eye. "He has these romantic notions about people and places. If you ask me, the elves over the water are nothing but a bunch of snobs, maintaining their position by belittling others. Unfortunately he believes that idiocy." With the bowls on the table, Malraux reached into another chopped-off stalagmite and pulled out spoons. "Times change, and those that can't keep up will be swept away." He looked in dismay at the table. "I forgot the tablecloth."

"Too late now," Aelvarim said, entering the chamber carrying an armful of flowers. "Where do you want them."

Malraux settled for tying the flowers into a single bundle and laying it in the center of the table. He indicated that Piper should sit by the decorative end and Aelvarim by the cut stems. The bench and table were a bit too low for Piper, but she managed to get her knees under the table without stretching her legs out straight. Aelvarim's feet appeared beside her chair, one ankle crossed over the other.

As Malraux retrieved napkins from another stalagmite, Aelvarim asked, "Do you believe in Fairy yet?"

"I think I'm dreaming." Piper accepted the napkin Malraux extended to her. She wasn't expecting him to pinch her arm, hard. "Ouch."

"You're not dreaming." Malraux offered a napkin to Aelvarim.

"Malraux," Aelvarim scolded. "I brought her here to convince her to help me find Grandmother Dickerson's murderer and save the story, not to be pinched and tormented."

"Got to be the husband or the butler," Malraux said, seating himself beside Aelvarim. "That's traditional."

Aelvarim frowned at him. "Grandmother Dickerson was a widow. And she had no butler."

Piper nodded. "And these days the traditional murderer is a boyfriend or lover."

They both stared at her, eyes wide and jaws slack.

Recovering first, Malraux whispered, "I think she'll do."

FOUR

AFTER WASHING UP, MALRAUX ASKED, "WOULD
you like to see my mine, where I work digging out . . .
stuff?"

"Work!" Piper looked around in dismay. "I've got to
get to work! I'd completely forgotten, I've got a job to
get to. What time is it?"

"Time?" Malraux shrugged. "Probably about noon."

He led the way out of the cavern and up the hill. The
thick forest of verdant trees thinned out as they climbed,
proving that the sun was high overhead.

Piper looked at Aelvarim. "I've got to get back to
Grandma's house."

"But I thought you wanted to see my home." It was
a statement, but Aelvarim said it as if it were a question.

Oh, yes. She remembered now. She'd planned on returning him to his keepers. Piper looked at Malraux, who
was looking at her expectantly. Unfortunately, Aelvarim's keepers were as crazy as he was. She was standing on the gentle slope of small, impossibly green
grass-covered, hill, looking down on a verdant forest of

a type never seen in Colorado. Well, when in Rome . . . "Sure. I think I've got time for that."

Malraux begged off, claiming pressing duties in his mine.

Aelvarim led her through dappled forest paths until they came to a stream. Here the water had carved deep into the forest floor, creating small cliffs on either side of the stream. Trees and shrubs clung to the tops of the cliffs, leaning precariously over the water. Piper guessed it to be about ten to fifteen feet from the top of the cliffs down to the stream. Rocks and roots exposed along the sides would allow climbing, but it didn't look safe. Aelvarim walked confidently to an enormous fallen tree. Someone had partially hollowed it and put up rope railings, so that it would serve as a bridge.

A small hill rose on the other side. At the top was a small, quaint, thatch-covered, white cottage. A faint shimmer in the air around it blurred and rounded the edges, making it look strangely out of focus. Aelvarim waved his arm, and half bowed. "My home."

There was great pride in his voice as he said it. It reminded Piper in many ways of Grandma Dickerson's house, picturesquely sitting surrounded by what appeared to be a forest. "Very nice."

Wildflowers ran riot over what would have been the front lawn. She followed as he led her around the small hill where the house stood. The stream split around the hill; Piper wasn't sure if that made it an island or not, but it gave a sort of moat feel to the stream. The bridge they'd crossed was the only path across the stream.

Tucked on the other side of the hill were a variety of berry bushes. Past the berries, the trees and shrubs thinned out. Piper could see a valley below them, marked out in the tans, browns, and faded greens of what she thought of as an ordinary Colorado spring. They appeared to be standing on a mountainside. Beyond the valley stretched a plain of patchworked colors, fading into the distance.

Piper's breath caught in her throat, as it always did when she looked out over gorgeous vistas. Living in a place, seeing it every day, made forgetting how very beautiful it was far too easy.

"Worth the walk?" asked Aelvarim.

"Yes." Piper couldn't help grinning. "It's wonderful." She'd forgotten he was there. His voice had reminded her that she didn't know exactly where she was. The vista below looked to belong to Colorado, but the overly green forest behind her was out of a fairy tale. Looking to the top of the hill, she could see his house, only now, rather than a small thatched cottage she saw what looked like a long house, made of sod and stone with a arched roof. It had the shimmer around it, and looked somewhat out of focus.

"Do you believe in Fairy yet?" he asked.

She smiled. Better to humor him, until she got home. And there was the strangeness with his house. The land he lived on. His friends. "Sure. Why not?"

He frowned skeptically.

"I really need to get home," she said, starting back toward the tree-bridge. Before she crossed she looked back to find a small, shimmering fortlike castle in the place where the cottage had stood. In all, she decided she didn't want to ask.

They saw no sign of Malraux, Larkingtower, or the fairies on their way back. Aelvarim pointed out the paths to her, showing her how to find her way and what landmarks to look for. He stood by the gazebo as she walked to the back doorway. "Mind the door. Remember to think clearly about where you want to go before you leave the house."

"I promise." She glanced back to wave at him.

"Piper?" Aelvarim was biting his lip, looking thoughtful, when she turned around. "I thought you said you were a writer, but you implied you had to go somewhere for work?"

"Until I get published, I work wherever I can. Aunt Nellie arranged for a job at Independent Books for me. It's a bookstore."

Aelvarim nodded. She waved, again, and headed into the house. Piper looked back through the screen door, but he was no longer standing by the gazebo. She snorted a laugh, shook her head at her foolishness.

The clock on the wall said it was 1:50. She had over an hour before she had to be at work. She headed for the bedroom. She lay on the bed, staring up at the canopy, trying to make sense of the day.

Perhaps she'd dreamed it all. It was merely a lovely dream, and she'd only just now awakened. Except that she was dressed already, in clothes, she realized, that weren't appropriate for showing up on the first day of work. She rolled out of bed and began sorting through her clothes.

As she stood under the shower, she wondered if whatever Aelvarim had was contagious. She'd never heard of communicable insanity, but it might be possible.

Not likely, she thought as she dressed in black slacks and a muted floral button-down blouse. Piper was still having problems believing Aelvarim was real. For one, he was far too good-looking; that mix of beauty and masculinity just wasn't natural.

Picking up her purse and keys, she reflected that she'd wasted the morning completely. She still needed to get groceries, dust rags, and cleaning equipment for the house. Clothes baskets. Boxes to pack books in. Lemon oil for the furniture. A vacuum sweeper.

Piper raced out the door, thinking of the roads she needed to take to get to Independent Books. She hoped they hadn't changed, or the bookstore moved, in the two years since she'd been there.

Independent Books hadn't moved, and the roads hadn't changed. Sitting across the street from the Foothills Mall, facing out onto a main thoroughfare, surrounded by restaurants, Independent Books had grown as the stores around it grew. It had expanded, adding on a trendy coffee shop, and a burgeoning used-book store, called the Independent Annex. Other than being larger than Piper remembered, it hadn't changed. And she'd managed to arrive fifteen minutes early.

Inside smelled of books and roasting coffee beans. Three register counters guarded the big, double doors. The counters had been set up on a six-sided dais, allowing the clerks working there to overlook the store and coffee shop. Five-foot-high bookshelves divided the large main room. Four small cheap tables and a myriad of chairs huddled by the coffee counter in the corner. A stand of large plastic plants separated the books from the coffee and snacks. Other plastic plants had been scattered throughout the store, possibly for ambience.

No one stood behind the coffee counter. A bedraggled, college-age, bleached blonde amazon stood by one of the registers. Over half a dozen bangly bracelets clinked against each other on each of her arms. All of her fingers had at least one ring, and her ears were pierced multiple times in rows going up the sides of her ears. She wore a short black-leather skirt, and bloodred-silk blouse. The tag on the pale blue, Independent Books vest over her blouse said, HARMONY.

"Excuse me." Piper consulted quickly with the business card Aunt Nellie had given her. "I'm looking for Mr. Martin Gumble."

The amazon nodded, standing on tiptoe to look out over the store. She extended her arm, bracelets jangling, to point to a spot midway back along the right wall. "In

History. Short guy. Balding salt-and-pepper hair. Face like a bulldog."

"Thank you.

Mr. Gumble did indeed bear a resemblance to a jowly bulldog, but he could only be considered short by someone very tall. Piper introduced herself.

He shelved the book he was holding, and said, "Come on." He pushed the cart to the registers. "Stock these, would you, Harm? I'll be in the back office." He led Piper to a plain door at the back of the store and waved her inside. A desk huddled in one corner, with two rickety chairs; the rest of the large room was stacked with boxes. He opened a drawer, pulled out several forms, and motioned her to sit at the desk. "Fill these out. When you're done just leave them there, get a vest from the bottom drawer, and come find me. We'll get you started stocking the shelves."

"Uh . . . Thank you." Aunt Nellie had said he'd give her a job, but Piper'd really been expecting an interview first.

"So, what's your relationship with Nellwyn Fletcher?" Mr. Gumble asked, sounding nonchalant, but looking nervous.

"Aunt Nellie? She's my mother's sister." Piper grew nervous at the sour look on his face. "I, uhm. Can I ask how you know her?"

"Nellwyn Fletcher is a one-third owner of this store, and a usually silent partner in the business." He turned to leave.

Ah, the boss's nephew syndrome. Piper cleared her throat. "If it makes you feel any better, she'd be more likely to harass me than anyone else."

Mr. Gumble paused as he left the office, long enough to say, "We'll see."

She filled out the paperwork quickly. Proving herself at work was nothing new. It came with the start of each job. But this was the first time she'd been the boss's niece, with a whole load of other baggage against her.

Surprisingly, the vests were neatly folded in the large drawer. Piper put one on. Its light blue color unfortunately didn't match well with her floral blouse. She left the office to find Mr. Gumble back in the History section, shelving books. He took her around, introducing her to the other employees that were working that evening, Harm and a tall twenty-some young man named Jim.

They seemed friendly enough. Mr. Gumble showed her how to shelve the books and left her with two boxes of books. It wasn't difficult, just tedious. She made quick work of ten boxes, filling books in the History, Biography, Philosophy, Psychology, and Self-Help sections.

After that, Mr. Gumble put her in the back office to sort though boxes of used books, arranging them into categories.

As Piper sat on the dirty floor of the office sorting boxes, the blonde amazon, Harm, came in. She wound her way through the stacked boxes to a refrigerator hiding behind a large stack of boxes. Then returned to the desk, carrying a brown bag. "He's got you sorting the used books? I hate that."

Harm set her supper out on the desk. The forms Piper had filled out had miraculously disappeared. They chatted casually, while Harm ate and Piper sorted.

As they chatted, Piper discovered that Harm was getting her master's degree in history at a local college. Harm's parents were military and had been stationed nearby when she graduated high school, so Harm had stayed for college here, while her parents had been transferred out to Alaska. She had two brothers and too many boyfriends to keep track of.

Piper told Harm a little about her family and inheriting Grandma Dickerson's house, but was reluctant to mention anything about handsome elves or her trip through Fairy that morning.

Later, shelving the used books she'd sorted, Piper thought about Aelvarim and her morning. It had been fun, in a strange sort of way, and Aelvarim was delicious to look at, but either it was all a figment of her imagination, or she was insane. Given a choice, she'd rather it all be a figment of her imagination.

She didn't want to talk to anyone about it either. She didn't want to appear insane. The best course appeared to be to pretend it never happened, forget about Aelvarim, never mention it to anyone, and get on with her normal life.

The image of her brother barefoot at the funeral, Aunt Nellie leading the wake in a drinking song, and the look Sherlock had given Uncle Clem's outfit drifted through her mind. A normal life. All she'd ever wanted was a normal life. She didn't need fairies and elves and wizards and dwarves messing it up; her own family already handicapped her. Piper pushed a book roughly onto the shelf. A shadow fell across her, and she looked up guiltily.

Harm's hand was groping for her shoulder, but Harm was looking away. "You have to come see this guy. He is unreal."

Even standing and looking around Harm, Piper couldn't see anyone that unusual. "What?"

"There's this guy in Science Fiction and Fantasy. Incredible." Harm had a good grip on Piper's sleeve, and hauled her to a point where they could look over the shelves at the Science Fiction and Fantasy section. "I could hardly breathe when he walked in the store. I didn't know they were made that good-looking. There."

Piper gasped.

Dark, dark red hair, a familiar profile, and tight tunic shirt—it was Aelvarim.

FIVE

"AELVARIM?" PIPER SAID.

He looked up from the book he'd been perusing and saw her. He was wearing the same skintight hide tunic, leggings, boots, and cape he'd worn that morning. His hat had been tucked in his belt. As he shelved the book and walked over, Harm said, "You know him?"

"Yes. He's one of my great-grandmother's neighbors. I met him this morning." Piper desperately hoped that Aelvarim wouldn't start spouting on about fairies and wizards and dwarves.

"Good evening," Aelvarim said cheerily, leaning against the other side of the bookcase from them.

He and Harm were both tall enough that they could easily see over the five-foot bookshelves, though Aelvarim was taller. At about five-four, Piper suspected that she appeared to be peeping over the edge.

Harm reached her arm over the top of the bookcase, bangles clanking, to extend a hand to him. "Harmony O'Dooley."

Aelvarim took her hand, and acting as if sweeping her

a bow, kissed it quickly, then released it. "Aelvarim."

"Are you looking for anything in particular?" Harmony asked, pushing her blonde hair back behind her ears. Piper watched Aelvarim blink when he saw all the earrings. Harmony smiled dazedly at him. "Can I help you find anything?"

"I was looking for Piper. But thank you."

"Excuse us," Piper said. She walked quickly around the bookcases and dragged Aelvarim away from Harm to the Mystery section. "What are you doing here?"

"I've always wanted to see something of the world of humans, beyond Grandmother Dickerson's house. And I forgot to ask if you would mind if I searched the house for the manuscript she was writing. So I thought I could just find you and ask you." Aelvarim shrugged, and bit his lip. "It seemed like a good idea at the time."

She wanted to throttle him. The Mystery section would be an appropriate place. It must have shown on her face, because he stepped back from her. Seized by a sudden inspiration that had nothing to do with murder—to her knowledge elves didn't drive cars—Piper asked, "How did you get here?"

"I walked out through Grandmother Dickerson's house and asked the first person I saw where Independent Books was. I hadn't gone all that far when a vehicle stopped, and the man inside offered to take me here. So here I am."

Piper stared at him. Hadn't his mother warned him about accepting rides from strangers? Did elves have mothers? Though in all truth she figured he'd be more of a peril to anyone who picked him up than be in peril from them. She glanced around. Harm was watching them from her vantage point at the register. Piper couldn't see either Jim or Mr. Gumble. She checked her watch. "Look, I have another hour of work, then I can take you back home. Just wander around the store and stay out of trouble." She started to walk away, but looked back. "And don't touch anything!"

Aelvarim rewarded her with a strange look. As Piper walked through the doorway to the used-book annex, she saw Aelvarim walking toward Harm at the register.

There went any hope she'd had of being able to hide his insanity from other people. Still, she reminded herself as she shoved books onto the shelves, it wasn't her job to protect him from himself. He was all grown-up. The boss of himself.

Piper couldn't help feeling pangs of jealousy when she thought of him talking to Harm. No matter how possessive she might feel about him, he didn't belong to her. Just because he'd returned, even after she'd tried to take him back to his keepers, didn't mean she owned him.

She wondered what he thought of her. Heading for the back office to get the last box of used books, she saw Aelvarim standing with Mr. Gumble in the Philosophy section, chatting. Before she could get out of the back office, she was ambushed by Harm.

"Tell me about him! Is he your boyfriend? A long-lost cousin? What's he like?" Harm took the box from Piper and set it on the desk.

"He's just . . . a neighbor. He came over this morning, I gave him breakfast." It was the truth, of a sort. However, Piper added, "We had lunch, and we're going somewhere after I get off work." She didn't think that the fact that the somewhere was back home was any of Harm's business.

"I knew it!" Harm crowed. "He is so cute, so delicious. I knew no woman would pass him by. If you ever decide you don't want him, let me know."

Like someone unable to stop prodding at a sore tooth in their mouth, Piper found herself unable to stop from asking, "Don't you think he's dressed a little strange?"

Harm's bangly bracelets tinkled as she stroked her ears. "I'm not about to say anyone else looks strange." She straightened herself, accompanied by her bracelets. "How a person looks is not as important as how they think and act."

"And you're just interested in him for his mind?" Piper asked.

"Good point. Does he have a mind?" Harm asked.

"One all his own." Piper reached for the box.

Mr. Gumble opened the office door. "Are you two finished in here? Ready to get back to work yet? We do have a business to run out here."

"He's her boyfriend," Harm said, with a knowing nod as she squeezed past him.

"Congratulations," Mr. Gumble snarled. He waved to Piper to hurry up.

Piper picked up the box and returned to shelving the books. Before she'd reached the bottom of the box a shadow fell over her. Beside her she saw tan pointed boots and long, long legs in tight blue leggings.

Aelvarim smiled down at her. "May I help?"

"No. You don't work here. You're supposed to be staying out of trouble." Piper shoved another book onto the shelf.

"I think I'm making them nervous."

"How so?" Piper asked absently. She had two books left to shelve, then she could break the empty box down.

"Every time I try to talk to Harmony she starts babbling. And Mr. Gumble is keeping a watch on me." Aelvarim stooped to pluck one of the books from her hand and examine it.

"You're far too handsome for Harm, and Mr. Gumble's cranky." Piper took the book back and put it on the shelf. Grabbing the empty box, she stood.

Aelvarim assisted by cupping his hand around her elbow, lifting and steadying. He sounded mildly surprised when he said, "You think I'm handsome?"

She knew she should have strangled him in the Mystery section when she had the chance. "More than passing fair," she said, trying to remember where she'd heard the phrase before. "But I wouldn't want to tell you that. You'd get a swelled head." She hefted the empty box. "Let me get rid of this, and I'll be back."

A grin lit his face. Piper decided she'd better get away before she couldn't help grinning like a fool, too. When she came out of the back room she found him looking through the Art section. Several women customers were positioned strategically around, pretending to be looking at books, but gaping at Aelvarim. Mr. Gumble had to chase two women out a few minutes later when the store closed.

Piper peeled out of her vest. "I've got to go."

Mr. Gumble held out his hand for the vest. "And take him with you. Be back tomorrow at ten. That's when we open."

"Yes, sir!" Piper tugged on Aelvarim's arm to get him moving toward the door. "I'll see you in the morning."

Outside in the cool dark, Piper led Aelvarim to her car. "Come on, let's get you home."

"Not yet. I came here to find clues to Grandmother Dickerson's death." Aelvarim hung back from the car.

"I thought you said you wanted to search the house," Piper said as she unlocked the car's passenger-side door.

"Yes, but first I need to learn what I can about the human world. Otherwise, how would I recognize a clue if I saw one?"

A clue. Piper couldn't argue with that. It would be helpful if Aelvarim could get a clue. "I need to run some errands, buy some stuff for the house. How about I take you with me?"

"Yes. Thank you."

Piper waited until they'd both buckled their seat belts

before she said, "And I'll let you search the house, *if* you help me clean it."

Aelvarim opened his mouth to protest, but closed it, surrendering gracefully.

As she drove around the mall to get to a light that would take her out to the main thoroughfare, Aelvarim asked, "What is that building?"

Explaining was too difficult, so Piper took him into the mall, as it didn't close until an hour after the bookstore.

He gaped and stared like a hick who had never been off the farm. Since most people stared at him, he didn't seem to think his behavior was anything unusual. He reached for a tree. "It's growing inside this building," he said in awe.

"After a fashion." Piper forbore to mention how the trees were stunted, and really hadn't grown there from seeds but just been transplanted from really large pots.

When they could hear the roar of the fountain, Aelvarim raced ahead. Piper found him sitting on the edge, dangling the fingers of one hand in the water, smiling in wonderment. He looked up at her, blue eyes wide, his fingers rubbing together, as if he couldn't believe that his hand was actually wet. "It's beautiful! I never thought it would be beautiful."

Piper looked around. She'd been to this mall and others like it many times, but now she could see what he was saying. The shiny gold and chrome, the clear glass, a bit of greenery, the play of line and color, the open spaces, it all could indeed be aesthetically pleasing. If only she hadn't known it was all a crass commercial attempt to get her to buy more.

At the end of the mall was the movie theater. Piper considered going in to see a movie, but she didn't have enough cash on hand to cover both of them, and they couldn't spare the time if they were going to clean the house later.

They headed back for the car as the mall closed. As Piper unlocked the passenger-side door, she asked, "So did you find any clues?"

Aelvarim whirled around to look at the dark bulk of the mall behind them. "I forgot to look." He turned back nervously. "Well, I did learn about things here. So . . ." He glanced back at the mall before he got in the car.

He asked for an explanation of almost every building they passed, seeming particularly fascinated with the elementary school.

Piper parked the car near the entrance of a twenty-four-hour grocery superstore. Inside she had Aelvarim push the cart. They walked down the aisles, with Aelvarim gathering stares, and Piper collecting mops, brooms, and dust rags.

"What is all this?" Aelvarim asked, looking perplexedly into the cart.

"I told you, we're going to clean the house." Piper put two bottles into the cart, one a pine-scented floor cleaner, the other a lemon-scented furniture oil. She didn't much care if their scents clashed; they were the cheapest and would get rid of the dirt.

Picking up the bottle of floor cleaner, Aelvarim said, "I think there's a bottle just like this, in the kitchen. What sort of potion is it?"

"Where in the kitchen?" Piper clutched the cart, stopping it.

"In the lower cupboard, by the parlor door, behind the books." He handed the bottle to her as she reached for it, to put it back. "Larkingtower never stores his books with his potions. He says they might get together and do mischief. I told Grandmother Dickerson this, but she said Larkingtower was an old coot who wouldn't know real trouble if it slapped him in the face."

"Listen to Larkingtower." Piper put the bottle back on the shelf. "That is floor cleaner. It should never be mixed with books. Is there anything else in the cart that's already at the house?"

Aelvarim looked dubiously at the contents of the cart. Picking out the broom, he said, "I think I saw one of these once, but I don't remember where it was."

"Leave it." Piper frowned down at the broom, thinking of how little she knew of Grandma's house and how familiar Aelvarim seemed to be with it. She motioned for Aelvarim to follow her.

When she figured she had enough cleaning stuff, she led Aelvarim through the seasonal aisle, skirted the electronics section, came back to break the mesmerizing trance the TV had put him in, and towed him and the cart to the grocery section. Piper started loading the cart with milk, eggs, cheese, cereal, bread, and heat-and-eat meals. Aelvarim followed her in openmouthed wonder, and they left most of the other shoppers looking at them in a similar manner.

As they pulled up to the house, the headlights illuminated the porch and a lumpy bundle by the door. It turned out to be a vacuum cleaner Piper's mother had promised to lend her. They carted all the stuff into the kitchen. Piper put the groceries away, while Aelvarim watched her.

"May we search for the manuscript now?" Aelvarim asked.

"We can do it while we clean. I'll start vacuuming the dust in the parlor, you find the floor cleaner in the cupboard."

Aelvarim opened the cupboard door. "Did you want just the floor cleaner, or any potion I find in here?"

Piper paused. "Why don't you search all the cupboards, pile the books over there in the corner, and pull out any bottle you find. In fact, just empty all the cupboards."

"Good thinking. I'd be sure to find the manuscript that way." Aelvarim began pulling stuff out of the cupboards with a vim Piper had rarely seen in housecleaning.

She left him to it and headed out to the parlor. She'd learned early on that dusting furniture was a futile activity, and she rarely engaged in it. However, the level of dust in the house left her no choice. She plugged in the vacuum, pulled out the hose and brush attachment, and attacked the dust. She'd finished three-quarters of the room when she felt a tap on her shoulder.

"Did you find the manuscript? Any clues?" Aelvarim asked into the quiet after she'd turned the vacuum off.

Not willing to admit that she hadn't been looking, she just shook her head. Truthfully, she hadn't seen anything other than books, magazines, newspapers, furniture, and dust. There'd been no sign of any manuscript papers. "Other than a manuscript, I'm not really sure what I'm supposed to be looking for. Did you find anything?"

"Just more potions. Do you think you could tell me what they are?" He motioned toward the kitchen.

In the kitchen, all the cupboard doors stood open, and a small path led through the stacks of books and rows of bottles. Piper grabbed a trash bag and began throwing away any old or cruddy-looking bottles of cleaner. Aelvarim insisted that she tell him what each was. If she could read the label, she told him; if not, he set it aside on the back stoop, so he could consult with Larkingtower on its arcane properties.

Piper decided his was a mild inoffensive insanity and let him have them. Together, they put the rest of the cleaners, the groceries, the small appliances, and miscellaneous items back into the cupboards.

"Aelvarim, I really don't think Grandma was murdered. The doctors said she died of old age. And I don't really know what we're looking for here." A sudden thought occurred to her—what if he were a thief, looking for hidden jewels and such? Her common sense righted itself. Then he'd be out of luck. Grandma Dickerson was much too practical and sensible to waste her money on jewels and such that could be easily taken. She wasted it all on books and knowledge, both much harder to cart off.

"I know," Aelvarim said grimly, lifting the cereal boxes onto a high shelf Piper would need a chair to reach. "Though I, too, am uncertain what we are looking for. She had a manuscript. I saw it. On sheets of yellow paper."

"Handwritten?" Piper asked. Now there was a clue to what they were looking for.

"Yes," he drawled. "I don't think Grandmother Dickerson was much interested in demon writing, or ghost writing, or any other magical writing."

"Thanks for the sarcasm. I meant she didn't use a typewriter or word processor for her manuscript." Piper started shutting cupboards.

"What?" Aelvarim asked.

"I'll show you my laptop later. To the parlor." She trooped in ahead of him. "The newspapers. Put them next to the garage." She set words to action; he followed.

Piper asked as they passed in opposite directions, "Is there any other little fact that might help me sort out what is a clue and what is not?"

"I don't know. I'll know it when I see it," Aelvarim answered at the next passing.

They paused on the porch after the last load of newspapers, panting to catch their breaths, letting the cool night air ease the sweat of their exertions. Looking out at the night, at the trees rustling and swaying in the shadows from the moon and the stars, Piper whispered, "Is Fairy real?"

"Is Fairy real?" Aelvarim echoed. "Is imagination real? Are dreams real? Are you real?"

"That's not what I meant." Piper paused, unable to think of any other way to say it. "Are you real? Do you have substance? Can you make a change, a difference, in someone's life?"

Aelvarim held out his hand. "I have substance. I am solid."

Piper reached for his hand. It was warm, and strong, with surprisingly smooth, supple skin.

He put his other hand over hers. "Our worlds are intertwined. The stories from yours mold and shape mine. The shape and actions in mine changes yours." He shifted one hand, rippling the fingers, her fingers followed the motion of his. "Changes in one making changes in the other, making changes in the other, making changes in the other, rippling on into infinity."

She looked up at him. The dark shadowed his face, but she could still see his blue eyes glistening. "I'd always heard that ideas had power. I just wasn't expecting it to be so concrete."

A flashing smile winked in the dark, and he released her hand. "Ideas only have as much power as people are willing to give them."

Feeling at something of a loss in the conversation, Piper decided to change the subject. "Let's move the books from the kitchen to the empty spaces in the parlor. Then we can call it quits for the night."

After the books, magazines, and papers were cleared out of the kitchen, Aelvarim bade her good night, taking the bottles on the back stoop with him. Piper watched him this time, until his figure was swallowed into the darkness between the trees.

Checking the time, Piper discovered it was almost three in the morning. She flopped into bed, after changing into her flannel granny gown. She fell asleep wondering how much of what she remembered happening that day had been really real, and how much seemed real only because she wanted it to be real. And if she might not, in fact, be going crazy.

SIX

PIPER WOKE ONLY WHEN THE SUN HAD REACHED
far enough into the room to disturb her. The kitchen was
as clean as they'd left it the previous night, but no elves
sat at the table. The parlor was less dusty, with a vacuum
sitting in one corner, but still no elves. Piper looked out
the front window. She could see stacks of newspapers
by the garage and her car in the driveway.

Out on the porch she could see it was a bright spring
day. A few fluffy white clouds wafted through a brilliant
blue sky, and a gentle breeze pushed and pulled at the
trees. The breeze made it more than a little cool, but the
sun would warm the day up later.

Perhaps she'd merely dreamed all of yesterday, as a
way of making the work a little more fun. Though according to her dream, she had to be at work in just over
an hour.

That part turned out to be real, as she discovered as she
walked into Independent Books. Harm was behind the
register. Today she wore all black, except for the pale
blue Independent Books vest, along with her bangly

bracelets and the multicolored plastic hoop earrings dangling from the sides of her ears. She waved another pale blue vest at Piper. "So, you decided to give us another try."

"Well, I like eating." Piper grinned as she caught the vest Harm threw, and put it on.

"Don't we all." Harm shut the register drawer she'd been filling with change. "We get a break from Mr. Grumble. Mavis Culver, the assistant manager, is in this morning." Piper wondered if she'd heard Harm speak Mr. Gumble's name right. Harm just winked, and turned around to shout, "Mave! Piper Pied is here."

Mavis turned out to be just shorter than Piper, with dark hair, dark eyes, and dark skin, and bustling with energy. Just the three of them were working that morning. Mavis sent Harm to work at the coffee counter and undertook to show Piper how the register worked. Piper hadn't figured it to be all that difficult, but it turned out to include more than just taking money and making change. The register was computerized. Piper had to learn how to look up authors, titles, and subjects, in case a customer had a question. And how to tell if it was in-stock or on-order, and how to do a special order for a customer. Mavis explained that out-of-print didn't mean unavailable.

Luckily Mavis said, "For now if someone wants something, and it's not in-stock, or it's out-of-print, turn them over to one of us. You can watch how we handle it. You don't have to learn everything in one day."

The morning passed much more quickly than Piper had been expecting. Harm was busy at the coffee bar most of the morning, but the majority of the customers just picked up a coffee and left without buying any books. Piper worked the register and assisted customers. Mavis had disappeared. Piper suspected she was doing secret bookstore stuff in the back office, like placing orders or sorting boxes.

Just before noon Aunt Nellie breezed in the door. She waved to Harm, while heading for Piper at the register. "Hello, Piper! How're you getting on?"

"Pretty good. I don't think I shortchanged anyone yet, and I've nearly cleaned two rooms at the house." Piper stepped down from the register's dais. "Can I help you with anything?"

"Is Mavis in the back?" Aunt Nellie asked. When Piper said she was, Aunt Nellie headed for the back office. "Keep up the good work."

Piper looked at Harm, who shrugged. In a few minutes Aunt Nellie was back with Mavis. Mavis waved her hand at Piper. "You go to lunch with your aunt. We'll hold down the fort here."

"Come on," Aunt Nellie said, as Piper hesitated. "Your mother, and Gleda, and Africa are going to meet us."

Aunt Nellie and Piper arrived at Flannagan's first and were seated in the dark side room. Piper picked up her menu from the green-tablecloth-covered table, to buy some time to think. She hadn't planned on spending this much for lunch. Aunt Gleda—an honorary aunt since she was actually Piper's first cousin once removed, being Aunt Nellie and Piper's mother's first cousin—arrived next. Piper's mom, Tuesday Pied, and Africa followed soon after.

"So how's the house shaping up, dear?" Mom asked.

"Still a bit of a mess," Piper admitted.

"Poor thing," Aunt Gleda added from behind her menu. "I think Grandma went a little dotty there at the end."

"A ninety-three-year-old woman is entitled to her eccentricities," Aunt Nellie said authoritatively.

"But all those books, and magazines, and newspapers." Aunt Gleda slapped her menu down on the table. "They couldn't have been doing anything but making more dust. I just don't think she could have read all of them, what with her eyesight and all."

"Well she certainly wasn't cleaning!" Piper's mom patted Piper's arm. "She had to have been doing something."

"Maybe she had a boyfriend she didn't want the family to know about." Africa winked at Piper.

Aunt Nellie smiled. "Maybe she had a whole stable of them, but probably not. Stories I heard said she was crazy about books from the time she was a little child."

"I heard she'd written a novel," Piper said.

The others stared at her. Aunt Nellie asked, "Where did you hear this?"

Piper definitely didn't want to explain Aelvarim to them. She wished she hadn't said anything. She shrugged, and said, "One of her neighbors told me."

"What's it about?" her mom asked.

"I don't know. I haven't found it."

"Great-grandma wrote a book. Cool!" Africa pushed her blond hair back behind her ears. "You'll let the rest of us read it when you find it, right?"

"Of course. But it might not even exist." Piper raised her hands in surrender. "Who knows. If I do find it, I might try to see if I could get it published."

"Oh! I like that idea," Aunt Nellwyn exclaimed. "Feargus was right, Grandma would have wanted you to have the house and all that went with it. How is your writing coming?"

"She's spent the last week dealing with Grandma's funeral, moving into her house, and getting a new job. Give her a break." Africa waved to Jorge in the other room. "Let's order. I have to get back to work in forty minutes."

After they ordered, Aunt Gleda said, "I bet it's a fairy

story. The one Grandma wrote. That was all she'd talk about the last several months."

Piper's mom laughed. "Remember how she said the dust kept the fairies away, because they couldn't stop sneezing. She said they'd sneeze and fly backwards into the wall."

"What was it she said she was doing research on?" Aunt Nellie drummed the table with her fingers for a moment. "The principle of an inverse effect on magical and nonmagical spheres or something."

"I heard thaumaturgic in there somewhere," Piper's mom said. "Feminine inverse thaumaturgy for . . ."

"Something like that," Aunt Gleda interrupted. "Witchcraft by any other name."

"Speaking of witches." Aunt Nellie grinned. "Or some similar word. Shall we call this meeting to order?" She leaned toward Piper. "We've been meeting weekly to swap stock tips, or other business news. We used to call ourselves 'The Cousins,' but with you younger girls here now, we'll have to find something else."

Piper tried not to look too surprised as her mother, her aunt, and their cousin proceeded to talk business like robber barons of the nineteenth century. What businesses were booming, which were falling, and what industries were best for investment, both short- and long-term. Because Mr. Gumble had told her, she knew that Aunt Nellie was a part owner of Independent Books; but apparently the older women at this table owned, or held a partnership in, several other businesses in town and around the state.

Africa leaned across the table to whisper, "I've been invited to these for a couple of months now, and I'm only beginning to understand what they're saying. Aunt Nellie says not to worry, I'll pick it up eventually if I'm exposed enough."

On the drive back to Independent Books, Aunt Nellie

lectured. Piper decided it was the price of being the boss's niece and of attending their business lunches. "Don't worry if it was confusing for you today. Keep working, keep trying to understand what's going on around you, and eventually you'll be able to fly around on your broomstick with the best of us. It's actually been more fun than I thought it would be when we first started this at your age. I do what I can to teach my daughters, but they're on the coast."

Aunt Nellie didn't seem to notice that Piper hadn't said anything or made any please-continue type noises. She just kept lecturing. "I don't want to offend you, but you've worried Tuesday over the years. All this roaming around, during and after college. We know you need to find yourself, but things aren't like they were when we were young. It takes a while to realize that money is power. And if you want to change things, you have to have power. Unfortunately, the way the world is now, you have to know who you are and where you're going before you step out on your path. Otherwise, you'll end up lost, somewhere you didn't want to be. Do you understand me?"

"Yes. I understand." Piper was glad she'd learned the only correct answer to that question early in life. Whether it was true or not was a different issue. When she dealt with her family, "I understand you" was necessary for peace and quiet. Otherwise, you ended up with feuds that could span continents and generations. None of them made sense anyway.

Having worked hard to make Aunt Nellie happy, Piper had little reserves left to change Mr. Gumble's frowny face. He looked at his watch, and said, "Sales associates are only allotted a half hour for lunch."

"I'm sorry, Mr. Gumble," Piper said, wishing Aunt Nellie had come in with her. "I didn't know she was going to do this."

He sighed, and had her start straightening the shelves in the used-book annex and putting misfiled books back where they belonged. She didn't stop moving until her watch showed it was six o'clock. Mr. Gumble waved to her from the register. "The new schedule is posted on the wall, next to the computer, in the office. Don't be late."

Piper checked, and discovered that she had to be at work at ten again tomorrow, to open. Thankfully, both Harm and Mavis would be there, not Mr. Gumble. It was his day off. She went home happy.

As she was driving through the streets of the development to Grandma's house she spied a familiar blue cape and hat, walking up a hill. She pulled over and leaned out the window. "Want a ride?"

Aelvarim trotted over to the car and got in. Today he wore an ivory silk-looking tunic that was every bit as tight as the tan-colored hide one, a pair of taut gray trousers, and the pointy-toed tan ankle boots. She kept her window down, figuring she'd need a brisk wind to cool her off.

Piper asked, "What are you doing out here?"

"Looking for clues and not finding much. Did you work at the bookstore today?"

She wondered what the neighbors thought of the crazy man, claiming to be an elf, investigating a murder, and wandering around poking into things. "Just heading home from there."

"May we search for the manuscript again?" he asked wistfully. "Perhaps it's in one of the other rooms."

"Sure, why not. You'll help me clean, right?" she asked.

"Of course." Though she noticed he didn't sound too sure of it.

"By the way, does dust keep fairies away?" Piper turned into Grandma's driveway.

"Certain sorts of dust, yes. Why?"

Piper considered that. "Maybe I don't want to clean as much as I thought." She got out of the car. "Any excuse is good enough to avoid cleaning, I suppose."

"What?"

"I'll explain while I'm heating dinner."

They started their search in the attic, a small, stuffed room. Old furniture, busted electronics, boxes of junk, and eight trunks filled the low-ceilinged room. A single bare lightbulb cast most everything into shadow. The room felt cold and stuffy at the same time, and smelled of old wood and mothballs.

To get some space to work, Piper and Aelvarim decided to try to take the furniture out to the garage. They each picked a piece to carry and started down the narrow attic stairway. Piper carefully set the old, busted kitchen chair by the garage door. "Let me open this up and see how much room we have."

The garage was empty.

Aelvarim carried the two small side tables into the open space. "Sufficient room here, I think."

"I can't believe it's empty!" Piper stared into the depths of the vacant garage. "I figured it would be as packed as the rest of the house. Grandma didn't own a car, so I figured she just used it for storage." Piper walked inside, turning in the open space, to look for anything hanging on the walls or ceiling. "I expected newspapers, and old magazines, and junk."

A few powder marks on the garage ceiling and a few strangely green stains on the walls showed someone had used it for something at some time, but not for storing a car, or papers, or junk. After Piper recovered from the surprise of finding nothing, not even dust, in the garage, the trips from the attic went faster. Piper figured she could sort through the furniture here for what was salvageable antiques and what was fodder for the landfill.

Aelvarim studied the powder marks, between fetching loads.

"A clue?" Piper asked lightly.

"Perhaps. Something strange happened here, but I don't know what. Maybe Larkingtower can help." He walked to a corner and crouched to examine something on the floor. Piper watched his trousers tighten and stretch. He brought her mind back to what she was doing when he said, "Here's Grandmother Dickerson's broom. I don't think it's useful anymore."

Piper peered over his shoulder to see the broom lying flat on the floor, its bristles scorched and handle broken. She reached for it, but Aelvarim stopped her hand from touching it. "Don't touch it, please. I want Larkingtower to examine it. I think someone put a spell on it."

"What? Here? In the garage?"

"Yes, it's very strange. Fairy magic often doesn't work properly in the human world. I don't know anyone who would try it. Not since . . ." He stood up beside her. "Leave it. I'll deal with it later."

Five trips later they'd taken all the furniture from the attic. Piper decided to leave the boxes for later, and selected one of the trunks.

It was large, rectangular, and black. On a small brass label in fine calligraphed script was "Connlan Dickerson." The lid creaked as she opened it. Inside the trunk were men's clothes from years and years ago. It seemed to Piper that the scent of Great-grandpa's pipe lingered through the mothballs and time. She found a scratchy brown sweater with mended elbows, that she remembered. She hugged it to her, smiling at her memories.

"Is everything all right?" Aelvarim asked, from where he sat next to another black trunk.

"My great-grandfather's clothes. I was just remembering him. He used to take us for walks and point out all sorts of things to us." Piper motioned to the trunk next to him. "What did you find?"

"Connlan Dickerson's clothes." Aelvarim picked up a pair of shoes. "Would he be your great-grandfather?"

"Yes. I'm not sure what to do with these." Piper checked the labels on the other trunks. Four were labeled "Connlan Dickerson;" the other four "Alfreida Dickerson." She looked around the attic. "They must all be Grandma and Grandpa's clothes. They're too far out of style to donate, but not old enough to be antiques yet. Probably be best if we just stacked the trunks along the wall and left them."

Aelvarim insisted on opening each trunk. A quick peek confirmed that they all contained old clothes. Piper made sure the one with her great-grandmother's wedding dress was easy to get to. She wanted to look at Grandma Dickerson's best finery later when Aelvarim wasn't around, and compare with old pictures.

Most of the rest of the junk in the attic ended up in the growing trash pile by the garage. They carted all the books and magazines from the bedroom to the parlor, making the parlor more cluttered than it had been previously.

Piper looked around at the precarious piles, wondering if it would be better just to get rid of all the magazines rather than try to sort them out. Beside her Aelvarim also surveyed the room.

"I'm not sure we should put so many books in one room. It might cause problems," Aelvarim whispered.

It was already causing problems. Two stacks had fallen over. Piper shrugged. "Maybe you're right. But the bookshelves in the bedroom are filled. I think having them all in the same place will help me sort through them."

"I'm worried they might have reached a critical thaumaturgic mass. I'm not at all sure about mixing the fiction and nonfiction. What if they swap pages?"

She looked at him; he was serious. "Is that a pressing problem where you're from?"

He looked down at her and frowned in reaction. "Magic from the world of Fairy has leaked into this house. And it will stay here even as the worlds of Fairy and Human are ripped apart. Someone was practicing some sort of spell in the garage. Someone murdered your great-grandmother." He pointed to the piles of books. "They have real power. I know you don't believe me, but they do have power. The fiction portrayals directly change the shape of Fairy, which then changes your world. If they should be able to slide directly into your history . . ."

"So you're saying that if an author writes a story with a different view of how elves look, you would change?" Piper asked.

"Yes. It has happened before." Aelvarim ran a hand through his hair. "Thank goodness for Tolkien. Before him elves were all short, ugly, nasty bastards. Snatching children, scaring people, and generally delighting in mischief."

Having found the reason he disliked fairies, Piper couldn't resist saying, "Like fairies."

Aelvarim folded his arms, and frowned at her. "We can't leave all this in one room."

"Fine!" Piper started picking up part of a stack of magazines. "Let's get all the magazines out to the trash heap."

"Are they fiction or nonfiction?" Aelvarim asked.

"Mixed. Even the newspapers and history books are partially made up." Piper headed for the door with an armload of magazines.

"It's already started," Aelvarim breathed. He rushed to pick up a large stack of magazines.

"Hardly." Piper jiggled the handle, and kicked the

door open. "Magazines have been mixing fact and fiction for nearly as long as newspapers."

After several trips to take magazines to the trash pile they'd gotten all the magazines and most of the newspapers out. Piper leaned against the garage. She could see her breath puffing out in bits of fog into the cold night. She was tired, tired, tired. Her watch showed it was after midnight.

Aelvarim paused beside her in the cold and dark. "Why won't you believe me?"

"Would you want to believe that your great-grandmother was murdered?"

"No. But why won't you believe me about the stories and how they change things?"

Piper looked up. His golden skin nearly glowed in the moonlight, and she could see the blue of his eyes even in the dark. "I'm tired. I'm just tired. Maybe I need to see it for myself, before I can really believe it."

He took her by the arm and escorted her into the house. Inside was warm and lighted and cozy. He steered her through the parlor to the kitchen. "We've done enough work for tonight. You go to bed. I'll head home."

She followed him out the back door. "Good night, Aelvarim."

"Good night, Piper." He disappeared into the shadows under the trees.

She heard a melodic laughter, almost a chord, around the side of the house. She followed the sound to the front of the house. The garage and the trash pile were hulking sinister shapes in the cold dark. A tiny figure with bee's wings flew at her from the dark trash pile.

"Figwort, what are you doing here?" Piper asked.

He laughed and flew in circles around her.

"You just had to follow Aelvarim, and see what he was up to. Didn't you?" She held out her hand, palm down, for him to land on. "Are you satisfied with what you found?"

"Not yet." As Figwort landed several other fairies flew out from the shadows by the trash pile.

Piper had a quick impression of tiny bodies and various wings, before a fine mist rained in her face.

"Sleep. And dream."

SEVEN

PIPER WAS SITTING ON THE WINDOW SEAT IN the parlor at Grandma's house. She knew that, even though the walls were bowed, and the room several times larger than she remembered it. Books scampered about, on cute tiny little legs with enormous feet. The books clambered over each other forming and re-forming mountains and valleys around the furniture. Several books danced in a conga line across the sinuous back of the conversational in the corner.

The seat under her shifted, and Piper realized she was perched precariously atop a tall stack of papers, reaching halfway up the window. Something was written on them, but she couldn't read it. She had to steady herself with her arms to keep from falling.

She was afraid of falling. Afraid of being buried in the moving mass in the room. All those books with those enormous feet, she was afraid of being stomped to death. The window behind her was firmly shut, so there was no escape there. She tried to think of some way out of this.

Aelvarim would know what to do about this. He'd help her, but she had no idea if he was anywhere nearby. She called his name several times. He didn't answer.

Figwort flew into the room, laughing. "Do you need help?"

Opening her mouth to say yes, she remembered that just before this Figwort had blown a mist into her face. "No thank you. You would probably exact some payment for any help you gave."

"And Aelvarim wouldn't?" Figwort zipped around the room, barnstorming just over the books, agitating them to make mountains of greater height. He flew back to hover just out of reach. "He would, you know. He helps you only for what he can get out of it. Nothing is free. In return for his help, he wants you to believe what he says and assist him in his duties."

"Somehow that doesn't seem as sinister as someone who would stick me on top of a pile of papers, in a room full of stomping, militant books, and then ask me if I need help." Piper waved her arms to keep her balance.

"Oooo. Temper, temper."

Figwort flew away to disturb and confuse the books again. Piper remembered about the dust in the house making the fairies sneeze. As Figwort flew back, Piper reached out to pick up a handful of dust from a nearby bookshelf. When Figwort was close she blew the dust at him.

A cloud of dust enveloped him. Figwort began to sneeze, tremendous sneezes, which sent him flying back into the bookcase on the far wall and stirred up a great wind. The stack of papers under Piper swayed and shook, and she fell into the writhing sea of clambering books.

Piper couldn't get her feet under her, so she tried swimming. A large tome passed by, climbing to the top of the heap. Piper latched on to it by the dangling ribbon bookmark, and it dragged her up out of the smelly, flailing feet. She pulled herself up onto it as it reached the top. The title on the spine read, *Feminine Matrices: Their Strengths, Weaknesses, and Uses.*

Standing on the book, she saw a doorway. She jumped to the top of the next book heap over. The top book's title was, *The Power of Imagination, from Fairy Tales to Philosophy.* Another jump brought her nearer to the doorway, but her footing was unstable. Three smaller books fought for supremacy there. She could tell they were fiction by their bright colorful covers, but she couldn't read the titles. She jumped again, landing on a history of art book, then launched herself at the doorway.

Having lost her bearings in the tumultuous mass, Piper had no idea which doorway she was jumping through. To her surprise she landed in the attic, near the black trunks. An old-fashioned full-length mirror stood nearby. She couldn't remember seeing it in the attic before. It seemed solid when she touched it.

A picture had been tucked in one corner. It was her great-grandmother's wedding picture. Grandma was smiling apprehensively, clutching a wilting bouquet in front of a beautiful white dress. Grandpa stood beside her, looking solemn and serious in his black suit, only the white-knuckled grip he had on a small plain book betrayed his nervousness.

Looking at the picture reminded Piper that the dress was sitting in the trunk, waiting for her. The lid squeaked as she opened it. Inside, beautiful white silk and lace spilled from paper wrappings. Piper lifted the dress from the paper and the trunk and held it up against her, turning so she could see herself in the mirror.

In the mirror she saw herself wearing the dress, and looked down to see that in fact she was. Lace surrounded the off-the-shoulder neckline, and smooth white silk trailed to her ankles. She looked back to the mirror, but it was gone.

Aelvarim stood waiting for her, his hand extended toward her. He was dressed all in white, from the white-plumed hat on his head to his pointy-toed white boots. His white tunic shimmered like his home, alternately seeming gleaming white and nearly transparent silver. It perfectly set off his burnished golden skin, shining black-red hair, and happy blue eyes.

Piper could feel her heart pounding as she placed her shaking hand in his warm, strong, solid one. He started to lead her toward a stand of trees. Two magnificently tall, gray-blue Colorado blue spruce trees stood guard at the entrance to an unnaturally green grove of trees. Scattered flowers added splashes of pink, red, and violet to the green carpet of grass within. It looked as if reality were guarding the entrance to Fairy, a harmonious combination.

Realizing she'd forgotten her veil, she broke away from Aelvarim and hurried back to the black trunk, sitting open on a wide swath of green grass beside the footpath. Inside was empty except for the small black book Grandpa had been holding in the picture.

Behind her she heard a tinkling chord of laughter. Piper turned to find Meadowsweet and Pasqueflower, each holding a corner of white lace veil, trailing it behind them as they flew away. Piper jumped up, running in pursuit. She reached out and grabbed the trailing edge of the veil.

Meadowsweet and Pasqueflower reversed direction, wrapping the veil around her. Meadowsweet let go her corner of the veil to fly up and tap Piper on the nose. "This is what he wants to see you in, silly human."

Piper looked down. The wedding dress and veil were gone. She was in the short, satiny, spaghetti-strap chemise she'd been wearing when she'd first met Aelvarim.

A deep chuckle surprised her. She turned to see Aelvarim smiling at her and looking like he wanted to devour her. He shook his head and put his arms around her. "They're wrong you know. Truly, I want to see you out of that."

His mouth descended on hers in a kiss that swept everything from her mind, leaving behind painfully brilliant light.

Piper blinked the sun out of her eyes, shifting herself to shade her eyes from the sun and ease joints painful from a night sleeping on hard turf. Gritty sleep-sand irritated the corners of her eyes. She felt stiff and cold all over, and a strange metallic tang added an extra unwanted spice to the normal morning fuzz in her mouth. Looking around she discovered she was in exactly the same spot that the fairies had ambushed her the previous night.

"Fairies!"

Getting into the house, she discovered that it was already after nine in the morning. She had less than an hour to get to work. Stumbling into the bathroom, she muttered, "Figwort, if I ever get my hands on you, I'll rip your wings off."

Only as she was running out the door, keys in hand, did she remember that it was Mr. Gumble's day off. At least she wouldn't have him standing, tapping his foot, looking at his watch as she hurried in.

She walked through the door to Independent Books at exactly ten. Harm threw her a pale blue vest. "Glad you could join us."

"I need a new alarm clock," Piper lied.

Mavis split the work as she had the day before. Piper spent some time pretending to look up information for imaginary customers, as practice using the computer. It helped her look busy while she was actually thinking about her dream last night. Particularly the end. Particularly Aelvarim.

He was certainly better-looking than any man had any right to be. Of course, she didn't know what the standards were for elves. Probably they had to be better-looking than even the finest human male.

Giving up playing with the computer, Piper tried straightening the shelves. All she could think about was Aelvarim. No matter what she did, she thought of him.

After a while she came to the conclusion that the portion of her dream including him had been nothing but wishful thinking. He'd never shown any interest in her, other than convincing her to help him with this supposed murder. Even when he had seen her in that nightshirt, he'd acted as if nothing were unusual or exciting.

Piper wondered if perhaps elves didn't experience the physical aspects of attraction. For all she knew he'd find that just as confusing as toasters and fast-food french fries. She couldn't remember much of elf lore.

She didn't see Aelvarim on the way home. Neither was he at Grandma's house. Irritated at her inability to think of anything else, she decided that if Aelvarim was out meeting her new neighbors, she, too, should get out and meet them. She walked out the front door trying not to think of Aelvarim.

Walking up the driveway, she noticed that the trees and grass were getting greener. Some of the small flowers had small buds promising colorful flowers later in the spring. The air wasn't as cold as she'd anticipated.

At the end of the driveway, where she'd expected to find suburbs, she found typical Colorado scrub with a thin dirt road curving away around a small hill. She walked down the road a bit, and came to an overlook, similar to the one at Aelvarim's house. The tan, gray, and light green vista looked as Piper suspected it had in the time before the suburbs were built around Grandma's house.

Looking off in the distance south of her vantage point, she located a spot that might have been Aelvarim's. There was a shimmer at the top of the hill. It was too far for her to attempt to walk on unknown paths. So she headed back to get her car.

The car was no longer in the driveway. The garage and the trash pile were still there, but apparently automobiles didn't exist in Fairy. It was just as well. Piper wasn't at all sure the shocks could take the bumps on the rough dirt road. She headed through the backyard to the paths Aelvarim had shown her.

Larkingtower's spire made a fine foreground showpiece for the sunset behind it. Piper skirted around the meadow and hill, staying just within the forest, hoping to avoid Larkingtower.

The bridges were free of fairies. Just as well; she hadn't forgiven Figwort or the others yet. She didn't stop at Malraux's cave, but headed straight for Aelvarim's. A spun-sugar pink, miniature, fairy-tale castle complete with towers, turrets, minarets, arches, walls, battlements, and any other adornment known to castles waited on the top of the hill. Piper approached and knocked on the drawbridge, but got no answer. She knocked again with the same result.

After looking around to make sure there were no fairies about, she called, "Aelvarim!"

She glanced back as she walked over the bridge. The house was now sunset pink–tinged rock, square and squat, with iron bars over the windows and doors. She hesitated by Malraux's cave. He'd seemed nice enough, but without her friendly native guide she wasn't sure of her welcome.

"Malraux?" Piper called into the entrance of the cave. A faint sound returned to her. She wasn't sure but it wasn't just an echo. Malraux appeared before she could leave. He was wearing his leather apron, stuffing his gauntlets into his pocket.

"Welcome. Come in. I was hoping for a visitor tonight." Malraux took her hand to guide her through the twisting passage to his home.

It was as she remembered, with most of the light coming from the fireplace. A few lanterns had been lit, one sitting near where stalagmites had been carved into a conversation pit. Malraux led her to it and motioned for her to sit in one of the chairs carved from the rock. It was surprisingly comfortable and warm.

"What brings you out here tonight?" Malraux asked as he settled into a stone chair across from hers.

"Actually, I was looking for Aelvarim, but he doesn't seem to be home." The flimsiness of her excuse embarrassed her. She had no real reason for seeing Aelvarim either.

"He's out in the human realm, looking for clues to Grandmother Dickerson's death." Malraux leaned toward her. "Have you found something?"

Piper squirmed. "No. But I wanted to ask him about the fairies. They ambushed me last night, and I had the weirdest dreams and was nearly late to work this morning."

"Fairies!" Malraux shook his head. "It's so hard to tell when they're being mischievous and when they're just trying to help." He jumped down from his seat. "Come with me. I can give you something that will help keep the fairies away, at least when they're only up to no good. Which, as I've said before, is often not that much different from when they're trying to help. And I'll get to show you my mine at the same time."

He picked up the lantern and led the way deeper into the cave. Piper suspected that the mine had at first been a cave, and Malraux was merely expanding it. Most of the walls looked natural, but there were sections that were obviously carved into the rock. Most of the natural-looking sections were more than tall enough for her to stand upright as she walked. She had to stoop to get through the sections that had been carved. Malraux probably hadn't worried too much about the comfort of taller visitors when he was hewing passages through solid rock. Several stairways led down and down and down.

The lanternlight illuminated wonderful colors in the nearby rocks, pink and purple and white and tan, with occasional blue or green streaks. The cavern maintained a cool nearly cold, temperature, which didn't vary as they descended farther.

They reached a point where picks, shovels, and a wheelbarrow sat waiting. Malraux hung the lantern on a hook sticking out of one of the rock walls. "The secret to this magic is that you have to dig the gems out of the rock yourself."

Taking one pick, he handed her the other and pointed to an otherwise-unremarkable spot on the rock. "Try there. I've been getting some good results from that section."

Piper looked dubiously at the pick. "I just swing it at the rock and out comes a gem?"

"Basically." Malraux swung his pick expertly at the opposite wall. The thunderous sound of iron on rock echoed through the cavern. A few more tremendous swings—which Piper watched while keeping her hands over her ears—and bits of rock, large and small, skittered across the floor at Malraux's feet. He picked one of the smaller ones up and brought it to Piper. "What do you think?"

She took it from him. Dull and unimpressive, it looked like a bit of rock to Piper. "It's a rock."

He laughed and took it back from her. "Yes. But cut right, and polished, it'd be a pretty nice emerald."

Peering at the rock resting on Malraux's palm, Piper asked, "So how will I know if anything I manage to break off is a gem or just a chunk of rock?"

"You break the rock. I'll tell you when you've got something." Malraux settled back against the opposite wall, out of her range, and motioned for her to start.

Piper swung the pick at the wall of rock. A little ping rang out, nearly echoing. The rock appeared unfazed. Piper tried several times without achieving even a crack in the rock. She turned to find Malraux sitting on a large loose boulder, trying hard not to laugh at her. "I've never done this before."

"Perhaps if you tried singing. Put yourself into a rhythm. I hear that's supposed to help." Malraux shook with suppressed laughter.

"Do you sing while you do this?"

"No."

"Then I'm not singing either." Piper tried a few more swings with the pick. A small dent appeared where she'd been striking the stone. "So do I really need to do this, or is this just an excuse to get someone else to fight the stone for you?"

"Maybe I just need the laugh," Malraux said. Piper frowned at him. He shifted on his boulder. "Actually for the magic to work you have to do it yourself. Though I do admit I wouldn't refuse any help breaking rock that was cheerfully offered."

Piper tried again. In between swings, Malraux said, "People are a lot like rocks. Whether they're human, elf, dwarf, fairy, or whatever. And I don't mean stupid. Necessarily. You often can't tell much about them until you've dug them out and polished them."

"How so?" Piper took the excuse to rest for a moment.

"Take Aelvarim, Larkingtower, and myself as examples. Things come in threes, remember. Traditionally, women are looked at as being one of three archetypes:

the maiden, the mother, and the crone. Most people don't think about it, but if you do, you'll see that men then fit into a similar set of archetypes." When Piper didn't respond he said, "The youth, the father, and the old geezer."

"Aelvarim would be the youth," Piper ventured.

"Surely you can guess who the old geezer is. From there it's not hard to deduce I'm cast as the father figure. Interestingly enough, throughout history there are generally only three generations of a family alive at any one time. Which is where I think the whole thing originated from, but I digress." He motioned for her to try the rock again.

A few futile hits later, Piper turned to ask, "So is there a point in all this?"

"Larkingtower and Aelvarim. Aelvarim suffers from wanting to be something he's not, and if you ask me is better for not being. Larkingtower also wants to be something he's not. In fact, I think he'd prefer to be anyone else but himself. Which explains his distaste for people of the feminine persuasion. These days elves are supposed to be tall, beautiful, powerful bards, casting spells with music, incurably high-minded, and hopelessly involved with grand epic adventures. Aelvarim falls short on several of those, or at least he thinks he does.

"Dwarves get to be short, bearded miners. We can only sing about gold, know everything there is to know about everything underground, can still decently wield a sword or ax, and are powerful enough in our own right. I fit right in, or well enough to suit me.

"Wizards, on the other hand, are temperamental, lazy, and afraid of women. Larkingtower has much too much energy to sit around all day, is actually rather sensitive, and secretly, deep in his heart, likes women."

Piper grinned at him. "Methinks the gentleman protests too much?"

"Something like that." Malraux smiled back at her. "So don't take his shouting or blustering at you seriously. The louder he gets, the more affection he's trying to cover. I caught him once taking some stew to Grandmother Dickerson, toward the end when she wasn't feeling well. He denied it, of course, and ended up throwing it out against a tree rather than be seen being nice. But why else would he be carrying a pot of stew on the pathway headed to her house? I've always been sorry I saw him. I think he planned on leaving it on her back stoop, anonymously."

Laughing, Piper tried swinging at the rock again.

Malraux cleared his throat. "And you?"

"Me?" She turned to face him.

"I suspect you also aren't happy with who you are."

Piper leaned against the cold rock wall. The flickering lanternlight cast unusual shadows on Malraux's face, but it didn't make him appear sinister, merely older and wiser. Piper sighed and turned back to make a thunderous swing at the rock. "I just want to be normal."

"And what is preventing you?"

She struck the rock hard again, leaving a spiderweb of tiny cracks on the wall. "Well, for starters, I'm in a mining cave, trying to dig out a gem, so a dwarf can put a spell on it, to keep the fairies away."

"Hmm."

Another mighty swing. "I'm helping an elf who swears my great-grandmother was murdered, even though the doctors say it was old age. Not that any of that matters. Even without it, I'd still be related to all the crazies in my family. My mother, aunt, and first cousin once removed have delusions that they're old-fashioned robber barons. They sang drinking songs at Grandma's wake. Most everyone in my generation hates the name their parents gave them but doesn't do anything about it. I guess that's what really bothers me. We don't, any of us, do anything about it." She swung once again at the wall, and the thunderous clang of iron on rock echoed through the cavern.

Bits of rock chunked off the wall to scatter at Piper's feet. She stared down at them in surprise.

Malraux patted her arm and took the pick from her. "I knew if you were mad enough, you could do it." He stooped to pick up a piece of undistinguished rock. "This should do nicely."

"Was Grandma really murdered?" Piper asked, regretting the whine in her voice and hoping he'd deny it.

"Most certainly. We can all of us feel the rift widening between our world and yours." Malraux pocketed the rock, and took the lantern from its hook. "Follow me, I'll show you where the rift has already torn at the fabric of Fairy."

Around and about, up one set of stairs, and through several corridors, Malraux walked, with Piper following in his wake. He stopped several times to show her black splotches on the rock, claiming they were holes torn into the fabric of Fairy by the rift.

"Don't touch them. They swallow anything that touches them." He demonstrated by tossing a pebble into one that was directly above them on a low ceiling.

It didn't arch inside just to fall back. It just ceased to be as soon as it touched the black.

"Watch out for them," Malraux warned, heading back for his home chamber. "If you see one, stay as far away as possible."

Piper nodded fearfully. Things were definitely getting too weird for her. She suddenly wanted nothing to do with any of this.

They were ascending the second stairway when a deep

rumble echoed through the cavern, and the floor beneath them shook. Dust rolled down in clouds from above them.

"Cave-in," Malraux whispered.

EIGHT

WHEN THE RUMBLING AND SHAKING STOPPED they hurried up the stairs. Around two curves, the corridor was blocked completely. Malraux headed back the way they'd come. "Maybe we can get around it."

He took Piper through three different routes consisting of a variety of rooms and corridors, both natural and carved, but all ended in a pile of rubble. Malraux started to lean against the wall. "I hate mining."

"Don't! There's a rift there." Piper grabbed Malraux's shoulder to stop him.

Malraux jumped away, turning to shine the lantern-light on the black hole on the wall. "These may be the cause of the cave-in. If enough of these form, they undermine the cavern's structure." He looked curiously from the large hole to the pile of rubble. "Looks to be just plain rock."

Setting the lantern down on the ground, Malraux climbed up onto the pile of rocks spilling into the corridor. Piper started after him, and he motioned for her to get back down. "I think we can dig ourselves out.

Hand me the lantern." He peered at the rocks near the ceiling. "Yes. I can see a passage through to the other side."

Working together they started moving the rocks. They pushed a mini avalanche of rocks down the pile. As a few clattered, rolling down the corridor, Piper asked, "If you hate mining, why do you do it?"

"Oh, well. I'm a dwarf. That's what we do." Malraux tugged at his beard and tossed a rock at the rift hole. "I'm actually not all that excited about digging out gold and gems and minerals. What I really like is making the chambers and stairs and corridors and stuff."

"Excavation and construction?" Piper used her feet to leverage a large rock down the pile.

"And art. I like making sculptures from the stalagmites and in the walls. I found this one chamber. It's huge. It could become a grand hall with some work. I only mine what I have to, so that I can spend time working on my creations." Malraux looked critically at the rocks around them. "I think we might be able to send a bunch of these into the rift. That would get them out of our way permanently." He sketched out a plan to send an avalanche down to the side where the rift was.

"What happens to them once they're in the rift? I mean will the holes eventually fill up?" Piper asked.

"No. Rifts never fill. Whatever gets into them just isn't anymore. It doesn't exist, not here, not anywhere. If something isn't done to stop them, they'll swallow all of Fairy."

They pushed hard, sending another flurry of rocks down the pile. Piper watched the rocks hitting the rift hole disappear.

Getting a small tunnel opened wasn't hard, but keeping it opened through to the other side was more difficult. Malraux crawled ahead, slowly digging out and passing rocks back to Piper, who tossed them down the other end of the pile.

They wearily walked into Malraux's chamber, collapsing on the stalagmite furniture before noticing Aelvarim standing by the fireplace.

"What happened? Are you all right?" Aelvarim hurried over to them. When Malraux started to stand up, Aelvarim waved him back to his chair. "Is there anything I can get you?"

"Get the mead. I'm tired and thirsty." Malraux fumbled with the ties to his apron, pulling it off and tossing it to the floor.

Aelvarim fetched a stone jug, putting it on the table beside Malraux, and picked up the apron. "What happened?"

"We were in the mine. There was a cave-in," Piper said, wondering if Malraux would mind if she just fell asleep in the chair, rather than attempt going home.

As he hung up the apron, Aelvarim asked, "What were you doing in the mine?"

Malraux pulled Piper's rock from his pocket. "The fairies have been pestering her. She said they put a sleep on her last night at Grandmother Dickerson's house, and she was late getting around today. So, I thought I'd make her a ward. Here's a gem she dug out herself. Would you mind? I'm tired."

Taking the rock, Aelvarim asked incredulously, "The fairies were at Grandmother Dickerson's house?"

Piper found the energy to nod.

"I don't think they meant any harm." Malraux picked up the jug and pulled the cork out. "But that doesn't necessarily make any difference in what they do." He drank from the jug, then sat back, hugging the jug to his chest.

Aelvarim had picked the rock up with a pair of tongs

and held it in the fire. "I didn't think they ventured that far."

"I didn't either." Malraux sat up, appearing recovered and energetic. He took one more drink and brought the jug to Piper. "Take one swallow of this. If you need more, you can have it, but don't get too much to start with."

"What is it?" Piper got the jug to her lips with Malraux's help. The mead tasted sweet and thick.

"The Mead of Vigor. Larkingtower makes it for me. Digging rock all day wears you out, even if you're a dwarf. I only use this on those days when for some reason, such as a cave-in, I've done more than I ought." Malraux took the jug back from Piper.

"Once or twice a week," Aelvarim muttered from beside the fire.

"Not that often," Malraux protested. He looked doubtfully at the jug in his hands. "Not usually. At least," he conceded, "not intentionally."

Aelvarim just shook his head, keeping his attention on the tongs in the fire.

Piper hadn't noticed anything when she'd first drunk the mead. Now she felt a sudden surge of energy racing from her stomach out to all her extremities. She sat up straight on the chair, while Malraux watched her.

"Do you want another drink?" Malraux asked.

"No. I don't think so." Piper touched the jug in Malraux's hands, amazed. "Will it keep me awake tonight, like caffeine?"

"It won't keep you awake." Malraux put the cork back in the opening. "But I don't know what caffeine is." He looked over to Aelvarim. "Is it ready yet?"

"Not yet." Aelvarim took the tongs out of the fire, breathed some words on the rock, making it glow red, and thrust it back into the fire.

Malraux supervised Aelvarim as he cast the necessary

spells on the rock. Malraux supplied a chain and jewel clasp for the small blue rock, and held the necklace up for Piper. "It's not cut and polished, we didn't have time for that, but it'll work all the same."

After putting it around her neck, Piper felt exactly the same. However, if the mead was any indication, this would probably work. She thanked them both. Aelvarim insisted on escorting her home.

Piper spent the next morning emptying Grandma's stuff from the wardrobe in the bedroom, since she only worked a short shift that afternoon. With every item she folded, Piper felt sadder and sadder. A small house, a few items of clothing, a few pieces of furniture, books, and miscellaneous things, could they really be all that was left of her great-grandmother?

Piper had expected to feel more of Grandma Dickerson's presence, here in her house, surrounded by her things. Why did it all feel so empty and forgotten?

Grandma had been wonderful, lively and witty, understanding and patient. Was there truly nothing left of her, not even a Grandma-shaped hole in the world? Would Piper's memories have to be enough?

Two trips got all Grandma's clothes into a partially filled trunk in the attic. Piper opened and looked into the trunk with Grandma's wedding dress, but didn't have the heart to pull it out.

INDEPENDENT BOOKS WAS A DREARY PLACE, between Mr. Gumble standing over her and her thoughts alternating between Grandma and Aelvarim. Returning home, she didn't see Aelvarim, again. She wandered the neighborhood, meeting a few of her neighbors, who seemed nice enough, welcoming and open. But she didn't dare mention Aelvarim, and no one else did. Eventually, she returned home and exited to Fairy.

"Four days ago, I didn't believe in Fairy," Piper muttered to herself as she walked through the beautiful green woodland. "Now I can't stay away from it."

She skirted Larkingtower's spire again, but the fairies were waiting for her at the first bridge. She'd just reached the top of the wooden arch of the bridge, when five fairies flew up to hover in front of her, blocking the path.

Figwort pointed accusingly at the blue rock on her necklace. "Why have you done this to us?"

Holding up her hands in a conciliatory gesture, Piper said, "While I realize you were just trying to help, I can't have you putting me to sleep whenever you feel like it. I have to get to work on time; otherwise, I'll lose my job." Not one of the fairies appeared to understand or sympathize. "Terrible things will happen."

"Terrible things are happening here!" Meadowsweet shouted. "The gaps are increasing in number and growing in size. How dare you!"

The Fairies flew off, but if Piper thought they were going to leave her alone, she was mistaken. They reappeared, flying around her, tossing tiny balls of mud at her. Piper tried dodging and swatting at them, it only seemed to infuriate them. While the warding necklace might protect her from their spells, it obviously didn't protect her from any ordinary viciousness.

Worse, they were driving her toward the meadow where Larkingtower's spire sat.

"You realize, being smaller than me and picking up the mud yourselves, you are getting dirtier than I am," Piper told them in what she hoped was a reasonable-sounding voice.

They took it as a taunt. Meadowsweet and Pasque-flower dived at her, snatching her hair, pulling it, and dropping her hair in her eyes. Piper couldn't seem to get her hair out of her face. No sooner had she pushed it back, but another fairy would grab a lock and pull hard. They managed to get in close to her, tugging at her clothes and pinching her.

A pebble stung her shoulder, dropped from above. Suddenly pebbles pelted in from several directions. One struck close to her eye.

"Stop that!" Piper flung her arms up, trying to protect her head and face.

Words, in a language unknown to Piper, rolled like thunder across the meadow, and the torment ceased. Cautiously, Piper peeked out, with her arm still protectively over her face.

She was standing near the spire in the middle of the meadow. Larkingtower stood nearby, his arms folded across his chest, his long robes and white beard flowing impressively in the nonexistent breeze. He frowned at her.

"Fairies!" He shook his head. "I suppose you're not hurt. Women always seem to scrape out of these little incidents unharmed."

"Thank you, no. I'm fine." Piper stood up straight. "And thank you for helping me."

"Bah." Larkingtower shook his finger at her. "You shouldn't be here, meddling in things of which you have no understanding. Leave here. Leave Aelvarim alone."

"I . . . He sought me out first," Piper protested.

"Stupid, meddling women." Smoke appeared around the edges of Larkingtower's robes. He appeared to grow larger, towering over Piper menacingly. "I warn you. Stay out of Fairy. You'll be our downfall. Leave here and never return, lest I transform you into a frog!"

Clouds gathered overhead, thunder rumbled in the distance. Piper shook with an unreasoning fear and fled toward home.

"Do not interfere in the workings of Fairy!" His words followed her into the woods. "You would only bring about ruin. Heed me. Meddle not in Fairy!"

As suddenly as they appeared, the clouds, thunder, and smoke disappeared. Piper found herself running through the woods toward her grandmother's house.

She stopped, leaning against a tree, panting. Reviewing her latest encounter with Larkingtower, Piper could understand Malraux's confidences last night. Larkingtower had helped her with the fairies. Thinking over his words, she realized his first concern was for her well-being, then for covering up his momentary lapse into compassion. She thought the smoke, thunder, and unreasoning terror were a little over the top, but then he might be a bit of a ham.

Still, she didn't think he'd appreciate it if she ever acted like she thought he was actually soft-hearted. She swore to herself to make certain she acted terrified whenever she was around him.

Wondering if he might be jealous of Aelvarim's ability to associate with, and even attract, women, Piper snickered.

At Grandma's house, she looked around the parlor. There was a lot of work to be done. Piper knew she should get started. Sort through the books, keep some, get rid of the rest. But the thought of the incredible mountains of books to be sorted through daunted her.

She hadn't written for almost a week. Deciding to leave the books, Piper set her laptop on the kitchen table and powered it up. She could start a new story. All she needed was an idea.

Waiting for inspiration, Piper remembered what Aelvarim had said about stories changing Fairy. Would her stories change Fairy? How much power did a writer have over Fairy?

Probably not enough to get rid of the rifts. If so, someone, Aelvarim, Malraux, or the fairies, would have asked her to take care of it by now. Maybe just writing wasn't enough. Maybe the stories had to go all the way to the readers, the more readers the more influence. She'd have to ask Aelvarim, or Malraux.

Her hand touched the blue stone hanging around her neck. It was warm. Could she change the fairies? Make them leave her alone without any warding? The only method of testing would be to meet the fairies without her necklace. She didn't want to take that chance. There was no telling what the fairies would do to her.

Fighting the fairies. That would make a good story. She needed a proper fantasy hero, tall, strong, handsome. But why would he be fighting the fairies?

Piper started typing. The hero quickly morphed into a thinly disguised Aelvarim. His counterpart had a certain suggestion of herself, but Piper ignored that.

Intent on her story, she didn't notice Aelvarim, until he was leaning over her shoulder. Reading.

NINE

PIPER CLOSED THE FILE QUICKLY. "WHAT ARE you doing here?"

"Larkingtower said that you'd been by, but had been stopped by the fairies. So I came to talk to you." Aelvarim pointed at the computer. "What is that?"

"This is my laptop computer. I do my writing here, rather than with pen and paper. I promised to show it to you, would you like to see it?"

Aelvarim leaned against one of the chairs, away from where Piper sat. "Actually, I was wondering what that story was, on that thing. Does it keep stories in it, like a bookshelf holds books, or how does it work?"

She pulled a chair up beside her, so he could sit down and watch. She showed him several applications on the computer, the spreadsheet, the drawing package, a few games, and the word processor.

His shoulder pressed into hers, and occasionally they would bump heads while looking at something. She hoped Aelvarim wouldn't notice how it distracted her.

Piper explained how her computer stored stories, and

that others could indeed hold books like a bookshelf. "I have a couple stories in electronic versions on this computer, but mostly I use this one to write my stories. I type them in on the keyboard, and they show up looking printed on the screen. It's easier to edit them using cut and paste than if I were to write them longhand. And, by attaching the computer to the printer, I can print them out and send them in."

"So the story that was on the screen originally, was yours?" he asked. "May I see it again and read it?"

"No. It's not finished. I was still writing it." Piper hoped that would be explanation enough.

"It was in free verse, yes?" After she nodded, Aelvarim asked, "Is most of your fiction, human fiction, in free verse?"

"Of course. Poetry often isn't, but most fiction stories and novels don't follow any poetic scheme." Piper was surprised by the look on his face; he seemed quite struck by this. Remembering he'd claimed to be a storysmith, she asked, "I suppose most of what you do is in verses?"

"It has been. It's the traditional form. But it's not required." He sighed and leaned back in his chair. "I've never been very good with poetry. I never seemed to have a knack for it. Perhaps I would be better off with free verse. Are there rules and conventions you follow even in free verse, or is anything allowed? It seems a slipshod way of going about it."

"Every genre has its own rules and conventions, what the readers prefer and expect. And different eras have had different fashions in writing. And of course, each writer has their own style." Piper shut the computer down and closed the lid.

Aelvarim sat quietly for a moment, appearing to think this over. His long fingers pushed his shiny dark red hair back behind his ears. "So how do you choose your themes? Why did you pick what you did for your story with the fairies?"

"Oh. Well. Uh." Piper fingered the lid of her computer. "I usually either let ideas come to me, or I use one that occurred to me when I couldn't write for whatever reason. Some people write ideas down, others just keep them percolating in their heads. Whatever works, I suppose."

"But what made you think of fighting fairies?" Aelvarim leaned close to her. "Was it your fight with them earlier?"

"In a way yes." Piper nodded slowly, reluctantly realizing she would have to tell him the truth. "I was angry with them. I just wished . . ."

Aelvarim stirred in his chair, looking horrified. "You must never, never, never try to make deliberate changes to Fairy. You can't know ahead of time what the ramifications of any change you make would be. The consequences would be beyond your control."

"I knew I couldn't change the fairies' behavior. I just wanted to be able to win against them, even if it was just in a story." Piper folded her arms and frowned at him. "I wasn't trying to make deliberate changes. I just wished I could swat them."

"Understandable. They're very frustrating." Aelvarim opened his hands in a conciliatory fashion. "I'm sorry I jumped to that conclusion. But it is something you need to be aware of as you write."

"So does that mean I can't write anything about Fairy?"

Aelvarim reached for her arm, touching her briefly with his fingertips, then leaned back. "No. Of course not. But you mustn't try to make any deliberate changes to merely suit yourself, or to gain a permanent advantage or revenge. You shouldn't try to change Larkingtower into a frog, or give Malraux the most fabulous mine ever. Like your great-grandmother, you have more power than you know." He ducked his head to face away from her. "I'm afraid with everything you do, every step you take, with all your power, that you'll attract the attention of whoever murdered your great-grandmother, and . . ."

Old age. She died of old age. Maybe if Piper kept repeating it. "I'm a big girl. I can take care of myself."

He smiled wryly and almost looked up. "That's what she said."

"She was in her nineties. Old age gets us all in the end." Piper wished she still believed it was only old age.

Sighing, Aelvarim shook his head. Piper saw his long-fingered, golden hands clasp and twist in his lap. She looked up as he turned his head to look at her. His blue eyes opened wide, and innocent. "Please be careful. Not only with your writing."

"Sound advice." Piper gently punched his shoulder. "You take it, too."

"I will. I must go now. Larkingtower has been taking undue interest in my comings and goings. He's very worried about all this." Aelvarim stood and walked to the door. He paused, and turned back, as if to say something more. In the end he just smiled and shook his head. "Good night."

"Good night, Aelvarim," Piper said, just before the door shut behind him.

She started to open her computer, but stopped with her hands on the lid, staring at it.

What was she going to do about him? Or better yet, about herself. She leaned back in her chair, letting her hands slide off the warm plastic of her computer, and looked at the chair he'd recently vacated. She could still see him there, in her imagination.

Tall. Handsome. Dark red hair. Big blue eyes. Warm molten golden skin. The top strings of his tunic slightly open. His hands resting quietly in his lap, strong fingers intertwined. A harp at his hip. Long muscular legs.

He was beautiful, and Piper appreciated that. But was he a crazy man, as she'd first suspected and now no longer thought? Or was he an elf?

An elf. From the realm of Fairy. Was she in love with an elf? A better question might be, was she in love? Could she love him, an elf, from a different world, with different goals, different dreams?

Piper walked into the bedroom and sat on the bed to think. Aelvarim was very beautiful, but he was also very unusual, very different, in a way she wasn't sure she could deal with.

And she wasn't at all sure he could love her back, if she did. In all, taking in his looks and who he was, he seemed unattainable. Was that her real motive in this? *I probably can't have him, so I want him.* Piper preferred to think she was smarter than that.

She knew she'd have to be blind not to be interested in him, but was that all it was? He was good-looking enough to make women stop in their tracks and drool. Was it simple, physical lust?

As much as she hated it she had to admit it was true. She felt a very strong physical attraction for him, but the thought of being linked with him in public made her cringe. What if he told someone he was an elf? Piper could almost hear herself telling someone, "Yes, my boyfriend is an elf. Job? None. Wealth? None that I know of. As far as I know he doesn't even own a car; doesn't know how to drive one. What does he do? He's a storysmith who hangs around in the world of Fairy with a dwarf and a wizard. He wants to be a poet, but he can't rhyme, can't do verses, and can't sing. But just look at him. Oh, boy."

Piper did love to look at him. She could have watched him all day long. But she was a responsible adult now, she told herself sternly. With a job and a house and everything.

Sighing, Piper got up from the bed and went back to the kitchen. She could just go on thinking that Aelvarim was attractive, he was, but she couldn't let it go any farther than that. He was from Fairy; she was real. Aelvarim could never love her, and Piper could never love him. They were too different.

She finished the story, changing the hero and eliminating the female counterpart completely. She saved it, closed her computer, and went to bed.

The next morning, Sunday, Piper slept in late. She had the day off work; the bookstore was only open for a short time on Sunday. She decided to spend what was left of the morning weeding the garden. The bedding around the scraggly stick rosebushes had very few weeds, but the flower beds around the gazebo, and the garden plot were thick with weeds. As she worked, Piper realized she'd need to get, or borrow, a mower.

She'd thought Grandma had one. When she'd had enough weeding, she decided to check the garage, opening the garage door wide to let the sunshine in. The furniture looked strangely cowed, huddled in the center of the garage, forlorn and rejected. There was nothing in the garage other than the furniture she and Aelvarim had brought down from the attic. Even the corner was empty; the singed and broken broom was gone. The stains remained on the walls and ceiling.

Piper looked carefully at the green stains on the walls. A faint sour odor clung near them. The highest was perhaps chest high, the majority waist high or less. They didn't appear to be scratches, but rather splotches, as if someone had thrown a liquid of some kind at the wall. Except in one spot where something appeared to have spilled against the wall and run down in long, separated drips.

The dark black ceiling stain looked just as if there'd been an explosion of some kind of dark powder. Gauging from the stain on the ceiling she located the center of the explosion, at approximately where the engine would be if a car pulled into the garage.

She was fairly certain she would have heard through the family grapevine if someone's car had exploded in Grandma's garage. Her family was weird, but not generally so exciting that explosions would pass without comment. Piper looked at the stains on the wall from her vantage point at what probably was the center of the explosion. She didn't think the green could be radiator fluid. Some might be green, but it didn't smell like that or stain like that.

What if it wasn't a car? Piper squinted, looking at the stains. If someone had a table right about here, higher than normal, like a shop table, and there'd been something on it that was green, say paint, and there'd been an explosion . . .

Piper couldn't remember anyone mentioning an explosion of any kind at Grandma's house, but if something had happened that Grandma didn't want anyone to know about, that could explain it.

Aelvarim walked into the garage. "Good day, Piper."

"Hello." Piper motioned for Aelvarim to come stand where she was. "Look. I've figured it out. There was a table here, and an explosion."

"Yes," he said smiling down at her. "Larkingtower looked in here yesterday. He took the broom to examine, but he said it appeared as if one of her paint cans burst, touching off the others, and causing a mess. He said she'd had a table in here where she kept her paints for the house. They and it are gone. From that and the markings, he drew his conclusions."

"Oh." Piper wilted. She thought she'd really been onto something there.

"Still, it's good to have the advice of two experts, rather than just one," he amended quickly.

"Who's the other expert?" Piper asked sardonically.

He had the nerve to give her his wide-eyed innocent look. "You. Of course. You know more about the human world than Larkingtower."

She was suddenly tired and hungry. "Come on. I need some lunch. Want to join me?" She headed back for the house.

"Yes, please. Thank you. I was hoping you would talk with me about your stories. Human stories. How do they write them?" Aelvarim followed her like an eager puppy, trailing just behind and to the right of her. Where she couldn't see his face, but could see his hands gesturing. "I don't mean on the computer, but . . . What are the conventions? How do they portray the story without verses?"

Approaching the house, it appeared even more like a face than ever. Except the eyes were angry and the smile a feral grin. She felt as if she were stepping into a wild lion's mouth as she stepped up onto the porch. She shuddered as she opened the front door.

"If you'd rather not . . ." Aelvarim said, bringing her back to where she was.

"No. No. It's not that." Piper ushered him into the book-cluttered parlor, and inspiration took her. "It occurred to me that perhaps better than me trying to tell you, you could read some for yourself." She opened her hand to the piles of books like a game-show girl showing off someone's just-won prize. "I think you'd understand it better then."

"Oh." He looked around the room, at first surprised, then excited. "Oh, yes. I'd like that. Which one? Where should I start?"

"Fiction, obviously." Piper headed for one of the stacks she'd carried from the bedroom. She knew what was in that stack. The others were a mystery to her. She looked through them until she came to a collection of fairy tales. It seemed appropriate. "Here, try this one."

Aelvarim looked at the cover and flipped a few pages, looking at the woodcuts illustrating the tales. "Thank you. I'll take good care of it. I promise. I'm sure I'll learn much." He grinned and flipped to the first page of the first story.

"You read. I'll go fix us lunch in the kitchen."

Piper left him leaning against one bookcase, reading. Only as she opened a cupboard in the kitchen did she remember that he'd had her read and explain the labels on the cleaner bottles.

TEN

PIPER SLAPPED TOGETHER TWO SANDWICHES, while she thought. She couldn't see any good explanation for Aelvarim to pretend he couldn't read the bottle labels, and yet devour the books on the bookshelves in the parlor. She didn't want to confront him. She decided to wait and see what happened.

Tossing a bag of chips on the table in between the two plates with sandwiches, Piper shouted, "Come and get it."

Aelvarim walked into the kitchen while reading the book. His right pointer finger slowly moved over the text as he read. His mouth moved silently, as if sounding out the words. His long legs shuffled without their usual grace in his attempt to walk without watching where he was going.

Looking up from the book, he smiled at her, and said, "I know most of these tales, but I've only seen them in verse. This is wonderful! I can compare what is in the book with the verses I know and see how it's done. Thank you."

"You're welcome." Piper poured two glasses of water and sat down to eat. "So, you're not having any problems with the book? You can learn what you need from it?"

"Oh yes. Thank you." Aelvarim set the book on the table, opened, so he could read as he ate.

Piper decided it seemed as good an idea as conversation at this point and picked a book out of the parlor to read herself. They read in companionable silence, lingering even after the food had been eaten. When Piper finally got up to clear the table, Aelvarim shut his book and helped her. He would clear his throat, or open his mouth, as if to say something, but remained quiet. Piper waited to see if he'd eventually work up the courage to tell her whatever he was thinking.

"Piper, could I ask a favor of you?" he said at last.

"Ask."

"Would you show me some of the places Grandmother Dickerson frequented before her death? Some human places?"

She sat back down in her chair. "I don't really know where she went, or what she did."

"Anything?" he asked, looking pitifully hopeful.

"Some of my relatives might know. I could ask them," she offered doubtfully. Maybe they'd think her questions were just part of mourning, or some such thing, and she could finesse her way past any mention of elves or Fairy.

Aelvarim tugged on her arm, to get her to stand. "No time like the present."

Alarm and horror spread through Piper. The thought of Aelvarim and some of her relatives actually meeting and talking scared her. The worst thought to cross her mind was that Aelvarim would probably fit in just fine. And some of her relatives would calmly accept anything he had to say about himself without blinking an eye.

"I don't think that's such a good idea," Piper started,

but he had her pinned with that pleading, innocent look, his blue eyes wide and golden skin glowing.

Next thing Piper knew they were in the car on their way to her parents' house. Like watching a train wreck, Piper found herself wondering with fascination what her family would make of Aelvarim, and what he would make of them. It would be interesting, if somewhat terrifying.

Her brother, Hamlin, opened the door of her parents' house for them. She made quick introductions that did nothing to take the suspicious and disapproving look from her brother's face.

"Everyone's in the back family room," Hamlin informed them reluctantly.

Piper led Aelvarim through the familiar, neat, uncluttered house to the family room. As they wound their way, the voices and laughter of her mother, father, Aunt Nellie, and Uncle Fletch drifted to them. The conversation stopped when they walked in.

"Hi," Piper said, waving to everyone. "I'd like you to meet Aelvarim. He's a neighbor of Grandma's. I met him when I moved in. Aelvarim, this is my mother, Tuesday Pied, my father, Emmett Pied, and my aunt and uncle, Nellie and Fletch Fletcher."

They welcomed him in. Piper's mother grinned madly as she waved the two of them to sit on a small, overstuffed, floral, two-seater couch. Aelvarim expressed himself eloquently, extending his sympathies on the loss of Grandmother Dickerson.

"How well did you know Alfreida?" Aunt Nellie asked.

"Not as well as I would have liked," Aelvarim said sincerely. "I have found her advice invaluable. She was always willing, and had the time, to talk to me."

Uncle Fletch stifled a laugh as Aunt Nellie dug an elbow into his side. Uncle Fletch smiled at Piper and winked. Aunt Nellie said, "She did enjoy a good talk, didn't she."

The conversation continued along polite, social niceties. Piper waited for someone to say something, or at least appear to notice Aelvarim's strange clothes, but everyone acted as if leggings, tunics, capes, and pointed boots were everyday, normal street wear. Only Hamlin, sulking by the doorway, seemed at all suspicious of Aelvarim.

"So, what do you do, Aelvarim?" Piper's mother asked.

Piper tried not to cringe as Aelvarim said, "I'm a storysmith."

"Our Piper here is a writer, you know," her father said, as if bestowing a great confidence.

"Yes. We've exchanged some ideas on storytelling conventions," Aelvarim said.

Aelvarim looked at Piper. She realized she must have had a sour look on her face, to match her thoughts, when he gave her a quizzical look.

"It's not like she's published or anything," Hamlin sneered.

Mom made a shushing noise and waved her hand at Hamlin. Hamlin glared at the ceiling for a moment.

"So how did you two meet?" Mom asked.

"He came by for a visit, at the house," Piper said quickly before Aelvarim could speak. She wanted to get the topic of conversation back to Grandma Dickerson. "Mom, I was wondering, do you know where Grandma might have gone to shop or just to have fun. There isn't that much to do in the subdivision there."

"She didn't do much shopping," Mom said, frowning disapproval at Piper. "Just groceries and whatnot at the superstore there by the highway. She kept mostly to herself. Didn't you say she was writing a book?"

Aelvarim leaned forward in excitement. "Yes, she was. Would you have seen it?"

"No." Mom looked confused. "Piper told us about it; otherwise, I'd never have known." She looked to her sister.

Aunt Nellie nodded, and added, "Piper told us. She promised that when she found it she'd get it published. Isn't that wonderful?"

She hadn't *promised,* she'd only said she'd look into it. Piper knew it would be futile to protest, so she kept her mouth shut. Aelvarim, meanwhile, leaned back on the couch, and said, "That would be wonderful."

"I've forgotten your last name," Dad said. "Might we know your family?"

"I don't have a last name. I'm an elf. I'm not sure if you'd know any of my family."

Piper nearly choked. Now she'd find out how her family would take that. The only one looking disconcerted was Uncle Fletch, who raised one eyebrow but kept silent.

Dad looked thoughtful. "My cousin married a dwarf. Said she was the best cook he'd ever met."

Aelvarim nodded sagely. "Most dwarves I've met are very good cooks."

"I never met any of her family either. I wonder if they're all dwarves," Dad mused.

"Most probably."

"Piper, why don't you come with me," Mom said. "We'll get snacks for everyone."

Bracing herself for what her mother might have to say to her in the kitchen, Piper didn't notice Hamlin follow them out, until he caught her arm in the hallway.

"Never, ever, let him get anywhere near my girlfriend."

"Don't worry, Lin. I have no intention of introducing

him to your girlfriend. You're safe." Piper wished she was.

"You and Mom and Aunt Nellie are all acting like twittering idiots," Hamlin said.

"We are not," Aunt Nellie said, gently smacking his head with the flat of her hand as she passed them on her way to the kitchen.

"Go be nice," Piper hissed at Lin, before heading for the kitchen. Her mother and aunt were putting together a platter of cheese, crackers, and vegetables.

"What a nice young man," Mom said. She smiled benignly at Piper and handed over the knife to cut cubes of cheese.

"He thinks he's an elf, Mom." Piper started hacking at the block of cheese.

"Well, he does look like an elf should," Aunt Nellie said, as she poured crackers onto the platter. "My goodness, but he's handsome."

"And he's a storysmith, too." Mom rooted through the pantry for another platter. "He's perfect. What are you waiting for, Piper?"

"Waiting for? Waiting for?" Piper stabbed the cheese with the knife.

"Yes. What are you waiting for?" Mom repeated as she held the second platter out to Aunt Nellie.

"Give the poor boy a hint, Piper." Aunt Nellie divided the crackers between the trays. "Let him know how you feel about him. For pity's sake, he's an elf, not a mind reader."

"Remember Uncle Jamie?" Mom shuddered. "He could read minds. I hated being around him."

Flinging cheese cubes onto the platters, Piper snorted. "That's impossible."

Aunt Nellie picked up the full platter and headed out of the kitchen. "You never met Uncle Jamie. We kids couldn't get away with anything when he was around. It was scary."

Mom picked up the other platter. "Be nice, dear. You've got a good one here." She walked out after Aunt Nellie.

Piper held the knife poised to stab something, but couldn't find anything to attack. She tossed the knife into the sink and stalked out. She could hear the voices and laughter drifting out to her from the family room again. Aelvarim's voice had a distinctive smooth resonance compared to the others.

From just inside the hallway she could see into the family room. Aelvarim was listening with actual interest to a story her father was telling, something she'd heard many times before. His blue eyes were intent on her father. He was actually leaning toward her father, the ties at the top of his tunic gaping open. The tips of his ears were hidden in his dark red hair.

Hamlin had warmed to Aelvarim finally. He was actually sitting on a chair nearby and had stopped looking sour. Her father had finished his story, and Aelvarim smiled while the others laughed gently.

Standing hidden in the hallway, she watched them for a few moments more. Aelvarim looked as if he belonged here, something Piper had always doubted about herself. Still, part of her was relieved they got on so well, but she wasn't sure why she felt that way.

As Piper stepped into the family room, Aelvarim instantly looked to her and started to stand. She waved him back into his seat and took hers next to him.

They were invited for dinner, and left shortly after the dishes were done. Piper wanted to get home in time to get to bed early, she opened at the bookstore in the morning.

"Thank you," Aelvarim said, as they stepped out of the car at Grandma's house. "I appreciate you allowing

me to meet your family and ask them about Grandmother Dickerson."

"Sure, no problem. I think they liked you anyway."

Smiling, he said, "I hope so. They're nice people."

"If you like that sort of thing."

Aelvarim looked suddenly around, frowning. "Larkingtower has been here, looking for me." He sighed,
irritatedly.

"He thinks I'm a bad influence."

"Don't feel flattered. He thought Grandmother Dickerson was a bad influence." Aelvarim stroked the harp
at his hip. "I must go. Be careful."

"You, too. Good night."

As she shelved books the next day at work, she
thought over how the afternoon and evening had gone.
Ambivalent best described her feelings. She was glad
things had gone so well, but disappointed that they had.
She wished she knew why he'd lied to her about his
ability to read. Or did he just think it didn't look elvish
to read cleanser bottles, but did to read books. More of
his crazy act, or a real foolishness? She couldn't make
up her mind.

Mr. Gumble stalked over to her carrying a medium-
size box. "Alfreida Dickerson ordered and paid in advance for these just before her death. Mrs. Fletcher says
they go to you since you inherited the house." He set
the box on the floor beside her. "Look through them,
and decide what you want to do with them. If you don't
want to take them home, we could probably make a deal
with you on them as used books."

Used books, Piper thought as he walked away. He'd
treat them as used books, and they hadn't left the store
yet. She opened the box. Inside were five books: a collection of Native American tales, a history of China, a
fictionalized history of the Russian Revolution, a lurid-
covered romance, and, the last, a mathematical textbook.

Piper peeked into the math book, wondering why Grandma had wanted a beginning geometry textbook. She could see no common thread among the books. Each seemed fascinating, except the math book, but why did Grandma order them together?

She carried the box to the register, and told Jim, "I'm taking these out to my car."

Jim waved at her to go. On her way back from the car, Piper wondered what other strange orders her grandmother might have made. And from whom.

Most of the loose papers she'd found in the house she'd thrown out. The garbage was due to be picked up today, so assuming it had been when she got home, she would have no old receipts to guide her. Perhaps there was some other way to find out what Grandma might have been buying in her last days.

That afternoon, as she took her turn on the register, she puttered around, searching through the computer. It took a while, but she finally discovered how to pull up an old order by asking Jim what she should do if she made a mistake and entered an order wrong.

Alone again, she searched for Grandma Dickerson's old orders. According to the computer, Grandma had made special orders about once a month through the bookstore, and had bought books on an almost-weekly basis. To the tune of about four hundred dollars a month.

So, Grandma had to have been dipping into her savings to get all those books. But why? Didn't she have anything else to do but read?

Jim spoke suddenly from beside her, making her jump. "The only other people who buy books like your great-grandmother did are writers."

"Writers, hmm," Piper said, thinking back to some of her own book shopping and the strange mixes of books she bought.

"Usually they're doing research for a story they're

writing, or planning to write. They also read like fiends."

"But if someone wasn't a writer, why would they buy books like that?"

He shrugged. "Don't know. There are a few people who're voracious readers, but usually they stick to one or two genres or subjects, like history and mystery. Every now and then, though"—he pointed to the computer screen with Grandma's orders on it—"you get someone that's just eccentric."

We should have put it on her tombstone. Just eccentric. Piper cleared the computer, wondering morbidly if it would be on hers when she died. There probably ought to be warning signs, rather like old-fashioned quarantine signs, to put up on the houses and cars of her and her relatives. Something to warn other people that they weren't dealing with the normal run of individual.

After she finished her turn on the register, Mr. Gumble had her straightening and reshelving misshelved books. She worked her way through the store, starting in the Children's section and ending in the Computer section. Most of what she did was returning books that customers had misplaced or just set down after deciding not to buy them. A small rolling book cart was kept at the register for such books that the customers would turn in before making their purchases.

Piper retrieved the cart and started reshelving the books on it. There was a good selection from Self-Help that someone had decided at the last minute to put back. One title stuck in her mind. It was *Feminine Matrices: Their Strengths, Weaknesses, and Uses.*"

Sounded like the sort of book that could have encouraged her mother and aunt to decide to emulate robber barons. Piper read the back cover. Sure enough it basically boiled down to creating a "Great Old Gals' " network to compensate for the "Good Old Boys' " network. Though nothing in the book would have been put so crassly and bluntly.

Giggling, Piper checked the author. Knowing her family, one of them might have written it. She'd never heard of the author, so probably they weren't related to her.

She picked dinner up on her way home, determined not to let the excuse that she was too tired keep her from starting on the tidal wave of books inundating the parlor. At least she wouldn't have to cook. She sat in the kitchen, eating slowly and reading, hoping someone would come by and give her an excuse not to have to tackle the parlor. Aelvarim never showed.

With no more excuses Piper finally slunk into the parlor to face the Herculean task of straightening and sorting the books. She intended to sort the books into various sections, reminiscent of the bookstore. She wished she knew the approximate percentage of fiction to nonfiction, it would help her decided whether to stack the fiction or the nonfiction in the kitchen.

Recognizing this as yet another delaying tactic, Piper ruthlessly chose to put the nonfiction in the kitchen and stack the fiction in the parlor. She started with the stacks on the furniture, hoping to be able to clear them off and actually use the parlor while she finished the cleanup.

After an hour or so she was beginning to believe Aelvarim was right about keeping so many books in one room. It made the job appear impossible, and if it didn't actually warp the normal world into the world of Fairy, it certainly seemed to.

She sat on the floor, looking at the spines of the next stack on the table. Halfway down the stack she remembered her dream, swimming in the books, and shuddered.

Feminine Matrices. She'd seen that title in her dream. Did it mean something?

ELEVEN

HAD THE DREAM ACTUALLY MEANT SOMETHING? Something intended to help her? Or were the fairies just up to some mischief? Coming across a title in the bookstore that had been in her dream could be nothing other than coincidence. Perhaps she'd seen the title during her previous straightening and not noticed it consciously. The dream merely pulled it out of her subconscious to put a title on a book in the sea around her, something concrete she could get a hold on.

Piper looked around the book-stacked parlor. If that book was here though . . .

She threw herself into her work with a vengeance, not so much to clean and straighten, but to see if Grandma had the books she remembered from her dream. She had to know if the dream meant anything. or if it was all coincidence. After the previous week she'd started having problems believing in coincidence.

None of the titles on the books covering the furniture had been in Piper's dream, but the books themselves were strange. She found several large, antique, leather-bound books purporting to be collections of magic spells. Three books were literary dissections of fairy tales, and a similar one discussed the ancient origins of European fairy tales. A particularly thick tome supporting a stack on one of the Queen Anne chairs was a collection of scholarly works, including graduate dissertations, on common themes of folk tales throughout the world.

The entire stack of books on the third, and last, Queen Anne chair were all devoted to New Age themes, particularly Wicca and spell casting. Piper leafed through a couple of the books, finding scrawled notes in the margin in a faint ballpoint script. She laughed to see some few dark scrawlings, most were "Rubbish!" or "Idiot!" But the lighter ones were usually references to another book.

Piper picked one of the references and tracked it as it expanded through several books. All the references contracted back to one of the spell books. Looking back over them it was obvious that Grandma had been tracking the variations and changes of a particular spell.

Clearly, from her selection of books and the notes she'd made in her books, Grandma had been researching Fairy and spell casting. For the novel she'd been writing, like Jim at the bookstore would suspect, or had she been up to something else?

Remembering the stains in the garage, Piper wondered if Aelvarim had guessed correctly the first time they'd seen it. Had Grandma been practicing magic in the garage and blown something up? Larkingtower might not suspect Grandma of that much initiative, considering his opinion of women. Or knowing his opinion, Grandma might have hidden what she was doing from him.

Looking up another reference brought Piper to a spell for hiding things. Grandma might have used it to hide her manuscript. Piper checked for a counterspell but discovered there was none. To cast the spell itself, the caster had to include a way for the object to be found. The book recommended that the caster put something such as the object becoming visible only under certain conditions, or only the owner with a concentrated effort being able to find it.

"Piper?" Aelvarim called from the kitchen.

"In the parlor." Piper quickly stacked the books she'd spread around her to look through. She stood as Aelvarim came into the room.

He carried the book she'd lent him yesterday. "I finished this and wondered if I might borrow another?"

"Look at this," she said as she pushed past him into the kitchen. "I think Grandma was studying spell casting, and Fairy."

"Oh?" Aelvarim followed her to the kitchen table.

She showed him what she'd found. Traced the hiding-objects spell references for him. "I think she may have used this to hide her manuscript."

"Yes. Oh, yes." Aelvarim excitedly flipped through the books again. "Now we can break the spell and find it."

"I don't think so." Piper sat tiredly in her chair at the table. "Grandma didn't leave any notes on how to find it. I mean, do we look only at the time of the full moon? Do we need an unbloomed rosebud in our hands?" She sighed. "My real fear is that she made it so only the owner can find it. Now that she's dead it's lost."

Aelvarim sat in the other chair dejectedly. "I don't think she'd do that. Or"—hope lit his face—"perhaps, since you inherited her house and all that goes with it, you are now the owner and can find it."

"So why haven't I found it yet?"

He blew out his breath and slumped again in his seat, in a very unelflike way. As he chewed absently on his lip while thinking, Piper was caught up in admiring him again. The blue of today's tunic exactly matched his eyes. The tan-gold color of his cape and hat gave his skin a burnished hue.

"Have you tried a concentrated hunt for it?" he asked suddenly, derailing her train of thought.

"What?"

"When you were looking, before I interrupted you, were you looking only for the manuscript? Or were you looking for something else?"

"Actually, I was looking for a certain title." Piper squirmed inwardly, feeling somewhat abashed to have forgotten the point of her search in her admiration of him. "I'd seen it earlier at the bookstore, and remembered it from my dream. So I thought it might be important, and I was looking for that."

"What dream?" Aelvarim leaned toward her intently.

"When the fairies put me to sleep I had this strange dream." She went on to describe the sea of books in the parlor from her dream, but left out everything after she'd escaped the books.

"What was the title of the book you were looking for?"

Piper told him. He leaned back, closed his eyes, and began to strum his harp quietly. He stood up and slowly walked into the parlor, as if dreaming. Approaching one of the bookshelves, he ran his fingertips along the edge of one high shelf. Plucking a book, Aelvarim extended it to Piper, saying, "Here it is."

She looked at the book in her hands—*Feminine Matrices. Their Strengths, Weaknesses, and Uses.*" In awe, she looked back to Aelvarim. She would never have recognized it. Unlike the book in her dream, it was an ordinary paperback, without any ribbon bookmark. Yet, with only the title to go on he'd found it. "Can you find the others, too?"

Aelvarim shook his head. "It's a very simple, very

basic, spell. If the Grandmother Dickerson's manuscript is hidden by her own ensorcelment, I probably couldn't use a simple locate spell to find it."

"No. I mean the others that I saw." Piper shook the book in her hand as if that would cause the other titles to fall out of her memory. *"The Power of Imagination, from Fairy Tales to Philosophy.* That was the other title. Could you find it."

He closed his eyes and strummed his harp again. Moments later he turned to another bookcase, crouched, and again ran his fingertips over the edge of the shelf. He plucked another book, handing it up to Piper.

Looking from the book to Aelvarim, Piper asked, "Could you teach me that trick?"

Smiling, Aelvarim stood. "It's possible. Do you remember any other books from the dream? They might be important."

"Only the cover illustrations, not the titles."

Taking the books from her and setting them sideways on a shelf, he said, "Close your eyes and concentrate on remembering the illustrations." Aelvarim walked behind her while stroking his harp, so that her back was against his chest. The gentle music from the harp stopped, and his hands caught hers, right to right and left to left.

Her concentration on the images from her dream was broken for a moment. She struggled to bring her mind back to the proper task. When she did, she felt suddenly compelled to walk across the parlor. Opening her eyes, she walked, dragging Aelvarim behind her. She didn't run her fingertips across the shelf, instead she dropped Aelvarim's right hand and reached unerringly for the book she wanted.

Aelvarim released her left hand and stepped away from her. "Now you try by yourself."

Blinking, Piper stared at him uncomprehendingly. "Try what? How did you do that?"

"Concentrate. And use your strength of will to find the book," he instructed her calmly.

"What about the harp? And . . . and humming." She waved the books in her hands. "How do you do that?"

His face grew flushed for a moment. "Music isn't needed for this spell. I merely use it to focus my thoughts. All you need is to concentrate on what you're looking for and will yourself to go to it."

Piper closed her eyes, bringing up the memory of the image of one of the other book covers from her dream. With a quick mental, "Here goes nothing," she decided to go to it. Nothing happened. She opened one eye; Aelvarim was watching her anxiously.

A quick smile flashed across his face. "Having trouble?"

She opened both eyes. "It's not working."

"How badly do you want to find the book?"

Closing both eyes, she tried again. This time she thought of how much she longed to read the book. An image of the book, up on a shelf out of her reach came to her.

Opening her eyes, she pointed to the highest shelf in front of her. "It's up there, where I can't reach it."

Tiptoeing on one of the Queen Anne chairs, Piper pulled the book from the shelf. "*Voilà!*"

Aelvarim took the book from her. She was looking down on him from her vantage point. His hair was thick and glossy, with the two cute little pointed tips of his ears sticking out. He turned his face up to look at her. "Would you try to find Grandmother Dickerson's manuscript? Please. If it's just hidden so that only the owner can find it, you should be able to locate it. You are the owner."

Piper stepped down from the chair before closing her eyes. She didn't know what the title was, or what it looked like, other than handwritten on yellow paper, or any other details. With that nebulous description in mind she tried thinking of how much she wanted to find it. She didn't feel compelled to go anywhere, and the only images that came to mind were from the dream the fairies had inflicted on her. Wearing the wedding dress, finding Aelvarim, chasing after the veil, kissing Aelvarim. Nothing helpful.

She opened her eyes to find Aelvarim studying her raptly. He was leaning toward her, one eyebrow raised in question. Piper just barely stopped herself from grabbing and kissing him. "Nothing. I don't have a title or an image to work with, so nothing happens."

He nodded, obviously trying to cover his disappointment. "It's getting late. You've worked hard all day. You're tired. Perhaps another time."

Piper didn't feel tired, but she let him leave anyway, before she made a fool of herself. She read late into the night. *The Power of Imagination* was a fascinating book.

Apparently the denizens of Fairy weren't the only ones who believed their world was enmeshed with the world of humans. This book described the effect of make-believe and what-if ideas on actual historical governments. The author talked about, and showed, beliefs' and folk tales' quantifiable effects on the behavior of their originating societies. In the last chapters, the belief of the author in the reality of the worlds of human imagination came through very clearly.

At work the next day, Piper surreptitiously tried the location spell Aelvarim had taught her, pleased to discover that it worked. She secretly used it twice to locate obscure books for customers, forcing Mr. Gumble to give her a grudging compliment.

After lunch, Mavis handed Piper a printed listing of books. "Here, this is for Philosophy. Take these and match the list against the actual inventory. I want to get an order in before the summer college courses start."

The inventory was easy. Piper merely checked off if the computer printout was correct, or entered a new number if the printout was wrong. She found only one copy of *The Power of Imagination*. She recognized a few other titles from her interrupted sorting of Grandma's books and wondered if Grandma had purchased them there.

In the back office she tried to hand the paperwork to Mavis, but Mavis motioned her to sit in the other chair next to the desk. "You read the books off from your list, and I'll enter the changes in the computer."

This division of labor went well, usually. Occasionally, Mavis would stop and send Piper to check another section for a book, in cases where the book's subject would fit in more than one section. Afterward they would continue.

"*The Power of Imagination*," Piper said. "One copy."

"What?"

"*The Power of Imagination, from Fairy Tales to Philosophy*. One copy."

"That's not on my list." Mavis frowned at her computer.

Piper walked around to look over Mavis's shoulder at the glowing computer screen. That title wasn't on the computer's list. She checked her printout. There it was.

"Show me the book," Mavis said.

They trooped out to the shelves, but the book wasn't there. Piper moved the other books aside to see if it had wormed its way behind the others. "It was right here."

Mavis took the printout from Piper, and scanned it. "I don't see it here either."

Snatching the papers back, Piper looked for the title. It was no longer there.

"Are you feeling all right?" Mavis asked, sounding very concerned. "You don't look too good."

Taking a deep breath, Piper shook her head. "I didn't

sleep well last night. But I could have sworn I saw that book, on the shelf and in the list."

"Come on," Mavis said, patting Piper's back and guiding her gently to the office. "We're both going cross-eyed looking at these stupid lists. Don't let it bother you."

There were two more discrepancies in the philosophy lists, but none in the History section they did next. For which Piper was eternally grateful. Mavis had begun to look at Piper worriedly. As Piper left, Mavis pulled her aside to whisper, "Get some rest and take your vitamins. You might be coming down with something."

Piper tried again to use the spell to locate Grandma's manuscript at the house, but failed. Discouraged, Piper sought out Fairy, to ask Malraux for help.

She passed Larkingtower's spire and the fairies' bridge without incident. The sound of metal striking stone echoed through the forest near Malraux's cave, so she knew well ahead of her arrival that he was home.

Aelvarim sat with his back to the path, on a tree stump, picking at the peeling bark, at the edge of grove of trees around Malraux's cave. In the center of the glade Malraux carved into a chunk of brown-and-gray stone with chisel and hammer. No definite shape had yet been formed, leaving Piper guessing what he might be doing.

"Good evening," Piper said.

The two looked up startled to see her. Aelvarim jumped up from his stump to welcome her. Malraux put his tools aside.

"Don't stop on account of me," Piper protested. "Keep going. It looks interesting."

"Just a bit of carving," Malraux said.

Piper sat on one of the larger rocks by the cave entrance. "You do wonderful work."

Malraux stroked his long beard, grinning with pride. "Just a bit of fun, that's all."

Aelvarim reseated himself on his stump. "She's right, though. You do wonderful carvings."

The dwarf looked from one to the other. "What are you two up to?"

"Nothing," Aelvarim said, all wounded innocence.

"The compliments were real, and deserved. But I did come here tonight for a reason," Piper said. She tucked her feet up underneath her. "I was hoping you might be able to give me some pointers on using this location spell. Maybe then I could find Grandma's manuscript."

Examining his chisel, Malraux said, "Aelvarim told me of your attempt at finding it last night. A location spell is the wrong way to go about it, I'm afraid. If Grandmother Dickerson used a spell to hide it, then a location spell would be useless." He set the chisel back down and looked at Piper. "Your best bet would be to use the ordinary talents and knowledge you have. I'm sure Grandmother Dickerson expected you'd be cleaning and straightening the house. That's probably when you'll find it."

"Sounds like you've found an excuse to tell me to go back to work and leave you alone," Piper grumbled.

Aelvarim flashed a grin and nodded before Malraux turned to look at him, and said, "She's talking like you now."

"I didn't see Larkingtower or the fairies on the way over here," Piper said to change the subject.

"Larkingtower is still there," Aelvarim said, quickly accepting the new topic. "He's trying various spells to hold off the growing gaps, but they don't seem to be working. Be careful on the bridge near his spire. The ground underneath it is riddled with holes." He added morosely, "No one's seen the fairies for over a day. We don't know if they left to find a safer area, or if they were swallowed by the opening of a rift."

"Have you found anything new?" Malraux asked

Piper. When she shook her head, he asked, "Have you found anything unusual?"

Piper told them about the books that had gone missing from the bookstore and the inventory lists. Malraux frowned and tugged at his beard as she talked. "That's an evil omen. Things are beginning to disappear from the human world. The rate of destruction will increase. Soon the gaps will show up in the human world. If something isn't done soon, nothing will be able to stop our worlds from ripping themselves apart, to oblivion."

Aelvarim stood up and motioned for Piper to follow him. "We should go now and search for Grandmother Dickerson's manuscript. We may not have much time."

"Wait." Malraux ran for his cave. "Let me get you something."

"Malraux, no!" Aelvarim shouted as he started after him. "Don't go in there."

Malraux waved a hand negligently as he disappeared into the cavern. Aelvarim stopped at the opening, looking in worriedly.

"What's the matter?" Piper asked.

"The cave is riddled with holes. It could collapse any moment. He promised he'd stay with me, and I assumed out of his mine, until this was over."

"Out of his mine, or out of his mind?" Piper whispered, too softly for Aelvarim to hear her.

Malraux appeared moments later carrying a wicker basket, with a patterned dish towel wrapped around its contents.

"A snack?" Piper asked.

"A bit of the mead. And a few things Grandmother Dickerson lent me, such as the basket." Malraux handed it to Piper. "You might find them useful in your search. You never know."

TWELVE

AT THE FAIRIES' BRIDGE NEAR LARKING-
tower's spire, Aelvarim walked cautiously, pointing out
spreading black gaps to Piper. The small stream had
been reduced to a mere trickle not much larger than what
could have come from a garden hose. Near the stream
a tree had fallen over; Piper started to walk across it, but
Aelvarim stopped her.

"No. That tree fell because a rift took its roots."
Crouching beside it, he carefully pulled aside the tall
stalks of grass to reveal an ugly black gap. "The tree
could shift anytime and slide into the rift. You with it.
Follow me." He led the way downstream to a point
where there were no black splotches marring the grassy
banks or the nearly dry pebble-strewn streambed.

They stepped across, and he headed back for the
bridge, motioning her to follow. "I'll show you under
the bridge. Be careful where you step and what you
touch."

Standing back from the bridge, Aelvarim pointed to
black stains on the shadowed streambed. "The rifts al-

most cover the entire area under the bridge now."

Piper missed the fairies. She wished they'd fly out at her, teasing and taunting. She even wished they'd throw rocks at her again. The stream just didn't seem the same without them. It was darker, more brooding. The rifts scarier without the fairies' chord of laughter to dispel the gloom.

"Stay back from there!"

Piper turned to see Larkingtower frowning at them.

"Do you want to disappear into a rift?" Larkingtower stalked over, his robes flapping around his ankles and his beard fluttering behind him like a flag. His staff pounded into the ground with each step. "She should not be here. She should not be meddling in this. There are dangers here even old elves don't understand and wouldn't confront. Too much for a fool human female."

Aelvarim opened both his hands to Larkingtower. "What is happening here affects her and her world, too. 'Twould be foolish indeed to reject her power and assistance because her form and shape don't meet with universal approval."

"Elves," Larkingtower grumbled. "You'd think they'd learn eventually. The only power human women have is to ensnare the minds and hearts of males and lead them astray." He turned on Piper, shaking a bony, gnarled finger in her face. "And don't think I haven't noticed you winding your wiles around him. You haven't let a day go by without reinforcing your net and tightening it about him. Distracting him from his duties, and muddling his attempts to mend this tale. You . . ."

"Larkingtower." Aelvarim looked distinctly uncomfortable, but while his mouth remained open, he didn't say anything else.

"Would Grandma performing magic spells have changed anything?" Piper asked, quickly filling in for Aelvarim.

"She attempted magic?" Thin tendrils of smoke curled out of Larkingtower's robes and beard. "That would change everything! Attempting the arcane arts without proper instruction is suicide. Madness, sheer madness!"

"We think that's what happened in the garage," Piper said. "We found some spell books, with notes she'd made. We think she may have hidden her manuscript with a hiding spell."

A mild evening breeze blew away the smoke from around Larkingtower. He looked pensively at the ground, his entire aspect changed, quiet and sad. "That would explain the singed broom." He sighed. "Poor woman. Why did she meddle? Why didn't she just leave well enough alone? Let someone who knew more make that decision?" Larkingtower glanced up from the ground to catch Piper's gaze. He quickly pulled himself up, as tall, straight, and haughty as he could. "Magical power should not be treated lightly. It is not something to dabble in or play with. There are aspects even the most advanced adept needs to be careful with."

Larkingtower blew out a long breath. It was as if someone had let the air out of a balloon. He shrank, until he looked like a stooped and gnarled old man, his beard and robes flapping loose around him, many sizes too big. He clung to his tall staff, as if only it was keeping him upright. "I'm tired. Go. Go both of you. It's been too much, too long, too hard. Go now." He turned and doddered slowly back toward his spire.

"Would you like some of Malraux's mead?" Piper stepped toward him, wishing she could help him in some way.

Aelvarim touched her arm, but before he could say anything Larkingtower looked back over his shoulder, smiling. "I have my own. I make it for Malraux. But I thank you."

"That was very kind of you," Aelvarim whispered as

he guided her toward the forest path on the other side of the meadow. "And very like Grandmother Dickerson."

"Poor thing," Piper murmured. "He seemed so sad, and so tired."

"We all are." Aelvarim pointed warningly to a black splotch sprawled across the path in front of them.

Piper didn't remember seeing any black gaps on her way through the forest earlier. She wondered if they'd spread this fast in the time she'd been visiting Fairy this evening, or there'd been fewer, but she hadn't noticed earlier.

They pointed out gaps to each other the whole way home. Aelvarim found the last one just outside the boundary of Grandma's yard.

"That's getting awfully close." Piper walked backwards, trying to see if any more would pop up as they walked. "Should I not sleep tonight? What if they come up and into the house while I sleep?"

"They won't. At least not tonight. And if they do, it will be too late to worry about them." Aelvarim glanced worriedly back. "When the rifts start taking over Grandmother Dickerson's house it will be too close to the end to stop them. The house is a strong connecting point. The rifts appear first in areas where the worlds are far separated and last where they are connected."

Deciding to fix a snack before tackling the book-filled parlor, Piper stopped in the kitchen. Setting the basket on the counter, she opened the dish towel to see what Malraux had sent with them. A miniature jug sat on one side of the basket. A small, old-fashioned candy tin turned out to be filled with rocks of some kind. A tiny sculpture of a fairy was wrapped in birthday tissue paper. The bottom of the basket was lined with three hand-crocheted pot holders in a green yarn shot with silver.

"What are these things?" Piper asked Aelvarim standing next to her.

He touched the rock-filled tin. "These Grandmother Dickerson said she'd bought in a store. She told Malraux she thought they were pretty, and asked what they were and if they had any interesting properties. They're just ordinary rocks, but pretty. I'm not sure why he still had them." His fingers caressed down the statue of the fairy. "Grandmother Dickerson admired Malraux's carvings, and asked him to make her a statue of a fairy. I don't remember what she gave him in return."

Aelvarim picked up the pot holders, smiling. "These are a joke of some kind. I don't remember how it started, but it's become a game. Whoever has them tries to give them away to someone else. The other person can refuse them if they notice them. I've had them twice. Larkingtower is always getting them. Grandmother Dickerson never refused them. She made them originally. Malraux is usually very careful to avoid them. I wonder how he ended up with them." He picked them up one by one. "There were four of them." He smiled at her. "If Malraux forgot one, you may be able to use that as an excuse to return the others."

"Grandma made these?" Piper took the pot holders from Aelvarim, holding them tight. Somehow they seemed to be more of a connection to her great-grandmother than the house and the books. She examined the pot holders. Some of the stitches were missing, even she could see that, but knowing that Grandma had toiled over each stitch made them special.

"I'll go start sorting books in the parlor."

Piper looked up to see Aelvarim giving her a strange look. "I'll fix a snack."

Once all the books had been sorted by subject, they began shelving them. Piper was determined to get all the books onto the shelves, even if she had to double shelve them. It was fairly mindless work, leaving Piper free to think.

"Do you think Larkingtower is all right? I mean, is he sick? Or, what do you think is wrong?" Piper asked.

Across the room, Aelvarim picked up a stack of books with one hand and put them on the shelves with the other. "He'll be fine. He's just tired. He's been staying up late trying to find a way to stop the rift. The spells he's tried haven't worked. I'm afraid he'll wear himself completely out before this is over."

Hesitating, Piper said, "I'm sorry if I'm disrupting your duties."

"You aren't." Aelvarim stopped to stand by Piper on his way to the kitchen to get more books. "This problem is too much for such as I, I'm afraid. You and Larkingtower and Malraux will have to make up for my inadequacies. The fairies are of no help to anyone. Unfortunately, no one else from Fairy will assist us, or in any way associate with beings from the Human world. It's just the four of us."

"Don't be stupid," Piper said. "You're certainly more suited for this sort of thing than I am. I have no idea what I'm doing."

He smiled. "Funny. Malraux says the same thing."

She waited until he returned from the kitchen. "You're the expert here. Don't forget it."

"I wish I were." Aelvarim pushed the books roughly onto the shelves, his long legs splayed for balance.

Piper made a trip to the kitchen for another armload of books. "All right. Let's think this through logically. You say Grandma Dickerson was murdered, and that is causing a rift between the worlds of Fairy and Human."

"Yes."

"When did you realize this happened?"

"Shortly after she died, I could sense that something

was wrong, some evil had transpired. Only later did I realize our worlds were moving apart."

"And it was accomplished by magic."

"Yes."

"Method, motive, and opportunity. That's how all the detectives in all the stories find the criminal." Piper put the last of her armload on the shelf, and turned to find Aelvarim standing still with a handful of books almost on the shelf. "Method was magic. Motive . . . Don't know. Opportunity. Who had the opportunity?"

Aelvarim stared at her amazed. "Anyone, I suppose."

"No. Not anyone." Piper shook her finger at him. "Think. It had to be someone near enough to put a spell on her. Someone that was around here, shortly before she died. And who might have a reason, however strange, to want her dead."

"The only people around here, as you say, were myself, Larkingtower, Malraux, and the fairies."

Piper let that sink in before she left to go get the next batch of books. Aelvarim followed her into the kitchen.

"No. No. It couldn't be one of us. We all loved Grandmother Dickerson. None of us would have a motive." Aelvarim appeared horrified.

"It's either that or someone from the Human world." Piper picked up another load of books.

When she finished that load and came back, Aelvarim was still standing there, looking horrified. She stepped directly in front of him, to break the path of his gaze.

"No," he whispered.

"Yes." Piper turned him toward the parlor and gave a gentle push. "Think it through. Opportunity. Someone nearby, with the ability. Who fits that description?"

She found him sitting in one of the Queen Anne chairs, bent over, with his hands covering his face. She shelved her load of books and put a hand on his shoulder. "Are you all right?"

His hands dropped to his lap. His face had the ravaged expression of one distraught beyond their ability to cope. In a rough whisper he said, "Who?"

"I don't know."

"I have been searching night and day. Larkingtower has been exhausting himself with his spells. Malraux has . . ."

When he didn't finish the sentence, Piper prompted him, "Malraux has . . . what?"

"Nothing," Aelvarim said despairingly. "He's done nothing at all."

Piper thought about Malraux. She knew so little of him, but he'd seemed so nice. Just like your average, next-door-neighbor serial killer.

Aelvarim grabbed Piper's hand as he stood and pulled her behind him as he stalked into the kitchen. "The pot holders. Where are the pot holders?"

"What?"

He snatched them up from the counter where Piper had left them, and, without letting go of Piper's hand, dragged her behind him as he headed for the garage.

"The explosion in the garage. There's something green on the walls. One of the pot holders is missing. What if the spell cast there wasn't cast by Grandmother Dickerson? What if it was the murderer, casting the final spell, and he needed something of hers? Something she'd owned and handled and even made. Something deeply associated with her, on her own property, even"— his teeth ground together for a moment—"using her belongings as ingredients, for his nefarious purposes."

In the garage, Aelvarim let go of Piper's hand, flipped the switch to turn on the light, and held the pot holders up next to the green spatters on the walls. They were a perfect match.

With a wordless cry, Aelvarim sank to the floor. "The

colors are the same. There's even small flecks of silver."
His free hand covered his face. "No."

"But what was the spell?" Piper took the pot holders
from him to make her own comparison. "When was the
spell thrown? Mom told me Grandma came down sick
one afternoon, went to the hospital, and died that evening. They said she just had indigestion and died of old
age. She was in her nineties." She looked down at Aelvarim, still sitting on the garage floor. "Well what do
we do now?"

"Now," Aelvarim whispered. "Now?" He stood up,
slowly and carefully. "Now. We need to figure out what
spell was cast. We need to know for certain before we
confront anyone. We must make sure Malraux really
perpetrated this evil before we face him. Then. Then, we
will have to fix the story."

THIRTEEN

WHILE PIPER SHELVED THE REST OF THE
books, Aelvarim sorted through the spell books, shelving
them as he finished them. He muttered to himself while
he worked. Piper would catch snatches of words. "Why
a pot holder?" "Couldn't be." "Something intimate."
"Beyond his capabilities."

Aelvarim finished his search before Piper finished putting all the books away. He helped her finish. The
shelves ended up holding double, and the outer row of
books hung off the edge of the shelf, but the furniture
and floor were cleared off.

"The location spell. Would you try it again?" Aelvarim asked, as Piper collapsed wearily into one of the
Queen Anne chairs.

"But Malraux said a location spell wouldn't work
against a hiding spell." She realized what she was saying
only after she said it. "Very well."

Closing her eyes, Piper thought of her great-
grandmother's nebulous manuscript, yellow paper, handwritten, subject unknown. This time she really, really

longed to find it. However, she still felt no compulsion to get up and go anywhere. She remembered the dream the fairies sent her and could only think how nice it would be to fall asleep now. She remembered the wedding dress and Aelvarim, but nothing helpful. Sleep sounded so nice. Someone gently shook her shoulder.

"Piper?"

She looked up into Aelvarim's wide blue eyes. His hand gently cupped her chin, and something cold and hard pressed against her lips.

"Drink. It'll help."

He held the miniature stone mead jug against her mouth, just beginning to tip it to pour some into her.

"You fell asleep on the chair." When she'd had a drink, he helped himself to a swallow. Gently, he chided her, "You have to concentrate for a location spell to work."

"Didn't Malraux give us that?" Piper asked sleepily. "Could it be poisoned?" Then she felt the effects of the mead spread from her stomach outward, like wildfire through her muscles. She sat up. "Maybe not."

"Most probably not," Aelvarim said, holding the jug out to her. "Firstly, he doesn't know we suspect him. Secondly, he doesn't make the mead. Thirdly"—he sighed—"I just can't see him harming anyone. Not us. Not Grandmother Dickerson."

Piper poured a large dollop of the sweet, thick mead into her mouth, and swallowed. "Then we're back to you, Larkingtower, or the fairies. You already ruled out the fairies. You'd know if you had. Though that may be why you haven't found yourself. That leaves Larkingtower."

"Or perhaps a wanderer. Someone we don't know, with methods and madness of their own."

"Know of anyone fitting that description? That was around these parts in the right time frame?" When Aelvarim shook his head, Piper added, "Well, Sheriff, arrest Malraux. He's our most likely suspect."

"There are many evils that wander and lurk. There is much to Fairy that you don't know or understand. Unlike the world of humans, just because something is unseen or unknown, doesn't mean it doesn't exist."

"Fine. Fine. Have it your way." The mead had done much to make Piper feel stronger and erase her tiredness, but her emotional weariness remained. The gloom and melancholy remained in spite of the electric strength flowing through her veins. Too bad, otherwise she might have been able to market it as a method of relieving depression. Piper looked around the parlor. "Did you find anything in Grandma's spell books?"

Aelvarim shook his head and lowered his frame into the chair next to Piper's. "No. The spells are not the sort that would cause an explosion. They're mostly building or helping or locating or hiding spells, which just require a bit of knowledge and an act of will. The few that require physical components aren't the sort to explode."

Her gaze traveled over the line of his long, muscular legs, and up his abdomen and chest, to the angles of his golden face trimmed by dark red hair. He was staring at the far bookcase with the spell books on it. His full lips trimmed into a hard line as he frowned.

He glanced over to her. "But then, that only confirms that she didn't cast the spell in the garage. Would you care to try again to locate Grandmother Dickerson's manuscript? Now that you're less likely to fall asleep."

Piper again closed her eyes and concentrated. Nothing. She opened her eyes. "Perhaps if I try walking around the house."

She walked through the house while concentrating. Again nothing. To be honest, as she walked around the house it was hard to concentrate on the manuscript. She had no concrete idea of what it looked like, or was about, and found the mess and work waiting for her distracting.

Aelvarim followed faithfully behind her, like a well-trained pup, a wide-eyed, hopeful expression on his face. Piper hated to disappoint him, but she was beginning to wonder if there really had been a manuscript. Or if the murderer had destroyed it.

They returned dejected to the parlor, to slump in the chairs. Outside the open window curtains, a predawn lightness shadowed the sky.

Eyeing the growing dawn, Aelvarim said, "I'd better be going. I need to talk to Larkingtower and Malraux. See if either of them saw any strangers lurking about before Grandmother Dickerson died."

"Be careful around Malraux."

Nodding sadly, Aelvarim walked out the door.

Piper saw him out, slept for a few hours, and headed off to Independent Books for her regular workday.

Mavis had Piper helping inventory in preparation for an order again. There were few discrepancies in the listings to trip Piper up, but she noticed that many books she remembered being on the shelves were missing, both from the shelves and from the listings.

Wondering if these were just not on the inventory lists and shelves of Independent Books, or if they were, in fact, no longer in existence, Piper asked, "Mavis, would it be possible to order a book called *The Power of Imagination, from Fairy Tales to Philosophy*?"

"Let me look it up." Mavis pressed a few keys on the computer, then entered the title. A few moments later, Mavis shook her head. "I don't have a listing for that as a book in print. How old is it? Perhaps we could do a rare book search on it."

"Never mind." Piper returned to her inventorying.

After lunch, Mr. Gumble had Piper cleaning, straightening, and reshelving the books. Harm asked if she could switch with Piper, since she'd been on the register all day, but Mr. Gumble refused.

In the Nonfiction Science section Piper saw a black splotch in the corner of one bottom shelf. Significantly, there were no books there. Unwilling to touch it, or risk setting a book into it, Piper searched the pockets of her pants. Pulling a penny from her pocket, Piper flipped it toward the gaping darkness. The penny arched through the air, glinting as it spun over and over. She more than half expected it would hit the shelf with a ping, and the black splotch would turn out to be nothing other than a bit of spilled paint. But as soon as the penny touched the blackness it disappeared.

Piper's first thought was to warn the others in the store. She stopped at the thought of the discrepancies between the lists and books she'd seen and what had shown up in Mavis's hands. Piper walked, trying to appear calm, to the register.

She smiled at Harm. "I thought I smelled something over in the Science section. I think someone spilled something. But I'm not feeling so good today. Allergies, you know. Could you go check, please?"

Harm happily bounded off to check. There were no screams, and she strolled back after a minute or so. "I didn't smell anything, or see any spills. Probably nothing."

The black rift sat malevolently where Piper'd last seen it in the corner on the bottom shelf. She resolutely continued her straightening. She found two more small gaps in Science, a good sized one in Math, a smattering of small pin-sized dots in the History section.

Mr. Gumble was shelving magazines in the Periodicals section, from a box he'd just opened. Piper watched in horror as he placed a stack of magazines on a shelf just as a rift opened up. The magazines disappeared. Mr.

Gumble didn't appear to notice. He moved on down the shelf with the next magazine.

The whole section was riddled with black gaps. Mr. Gumble not only didn't seem to notice them, he continued blithely on as books disappeared around him. She gasped when he touched one of the yawning rifts.

He turned to look at her. "Are you all right?"

"Yes. Yes, I'm fine." She looked at the misfiled magazine she'd brought over to put back. Piper couldn't put the poor innocent magazine on the shelf to disappear into a rift. "I . . . I'm fine."

"You look awfully pale."

"Allergies." Piper wandered away. She stashed the magazine in the Philosophy section.

Why hadn't Mr. Gumble disappeared when he touched the gap like everything else did? Was it because he couldn't see them? Did that mean he'd be safe from them? Did they not exist for him because he couldn't see them? If that were so, then probably all the other employees in the bookstore were safe. Harm hadn't seen the black gaps, Mr. Gumble hadn't seen them, Mavis hadn't seen them.

That didn't bode well for her own safety. Would the Human world continue apart from Fairy? Or would just those parts that didn't concern themselves with Fairy continue?

No, that was wrong. Aelvarim had said that the part of their worlds farthest apart would be affected first, and the points where they connected last.

Were they safe here for now because everyone in the store had some connection to Fairy? Piper didn't want to gamble with something like that, but she couldn't think of any excuse to evacuate the bookstore and keep it empty for the rest of the day.

"Are you feeling well?" Mavis had snuck up on Piper from behind. "You do look pale."

"I'm fine," Piper said automatically, then thought the better of it. "I think."

"She said it was allergies earlier," said Harm, walking up beside Mavis. "She said she thought she smelled something in the Science section. Someone might have spilled something, or something."

Mavis nodded crisply at Harm. "Wait here." She walked off toward the Science section.

"Grumble was worried about you," Harm explained. "He thought it might be, you know, female stuff."

Piper squelched an exclamation of frustration and settled for a quick examination of the ceiling.

When Mavis returned she, too, shook her head. "Nothing there. Are you sure you're feeling all right?"

At that moment Piper's cousin, Africa, breezed in and walked right up to them. "My goodness, Piper. You look like you've seen a ghost. Are you feeling all right?"

Over Piper's protestations, Mavis made arrangements to send Piper home. Africa called back to her office and took the rest of the day off. She insisted on seeing that Piper got home safe and sound.

Africa steered Piper out of the store. "Are you sure you're up to driving home?"

"Yes, I'm sure. I can drive home."

She opened Piper's door. "Okay, but I'm following you all the way. Don't try to lose me."

"I don't need a nanny," Piper complained as she sat in her driver's seat. "I promise I'll go right home and take care of myself."

Leaning down, Africa's blonde curls fell danglingly over the window trim of the car. She whispered, "Yes, I'm sure. But I want to hear all about this Aelvarim. The elf."

FOURTEEN

AELVARIM, THE ELF. PIPER DIDN'T KNOW WHO she wanted to strangle first, her mother, her aunt, Africa, or Aelvarim. She couldn't stand Africa's sly knowing smile glaring in the bright afternoon sun. "Follow me to Grandma's house. We can talk there."

Keeping track of Africa's car in the rearview mirror, Piper drove home. After seeing the change in the parlor, with the furniture cleared off and all the books shelved, Africa insisted on touring the house, to see what Piper had been doing, before she settled into one of the chairs in the parlor.

A puff of dust rose from the old burgundy-and-blue cushion of the Queen Anne chair as Africa sat. The place might be straightened, but it still needed to be cleaned. Piper wondered if she'd ever get the chance, between work and investigating who murdered Grandma.

"Now, tell me about this Aelvarim."

Piper collapsed into one of the chairs, raising another puff of dust that went circling and twinkling through the stream of sunlight coming in the window. Piper wondered what she should do about the gaps appearing in the Human world. She didn't have time to chitchat about silly handsome elves who showed up unexpectedly in the kitchen and turned everything upside down. "Oh, well. He's one of Grandma's neighbors. I met him the day after I moved in here."

Africa made a "more" motion with her hands, stirring the floating dust a bit.

"Tall, dark, handsome. Nice personality. I don't know. What do you want to know about him?"

"What I want to know is what you think about him. Is this serious? I mean, do you think he might be the one?" Africa scooted to the edge of her seat, fingering the worn rounded edge of the wooden trim around the seat of the chair.

"Africa, the man is . . . He thinks he's an elf. He dresses like a refugee from a Renaissance fair. He has these big blue eyes, and dark red hair that looks almost black, and little pointy ears. And he carries a harp. And . . ."

Smiling, Africa cooed, "So you like him?"

"There isn't a woman alive that wouldn't drool over him." Piper sat up and rubbed her temples. She had a headache, from fear and weariness. "But I'm afraid he might be terminally loony. And it may be catching." And it may be dangerous.

"So, you think he's an elf, too?"

Yes. I think he's an elf. I believe in Fairy. And I'm in way over my head. But Piper didn't say any of that, she wasn't about to tell Africa that. She settled for just giving Africa a strong look.

"You don't care what he may or may not be, as long as you can drool, or perhaps more than just drool?" Africa said, and snickered.

"I don't think he is interested in me that way." Piper slouched back into her chair, still rubbing her temples.

"Poor thing. I forgot, you're not feeling well. I should let you go get some rest." Africa leaned over to pat Piper's knee encouragingly. "Do you need anything? Is there anything I can get you?"

Just to be alone. "No."

"All right. You go get some rest." Africa stood and shook her finger at Piper. "But I want to meet this elf of yours. He sounds very interesting." She glanced at the door. "Any chance he'll be by soon?"

"No. He's at work," Piper lied. For all she knew Aelvarim could walk through any minute. She, too, watched the door, and noticed that the painted frame around the door was loose and needed to be nailed back down. A quick look around the room confirmed that there were no black gaps opening into nothingness in the parlor, but Piper expected them at any moment.

"What sort of work does an elf do?" Africa asked.

"He's a storysmith."

"That doesn't sound like a job with regular hours." Africa looked hopefully at the door, but no one knocked or came in.

"How about I have you and Sherlock over for dinner to meet him sometime?" Piper asked. Anything to get rid of her now.

"Sure." Africa brightened. "How about tonight?"

"Not tonight." Piper scrubbed her face with her hands. She had to do something about this headache. And the gaping black holes appearing everywhere. "Tomorrow night."

As soon as she was sure Africa was gone, Piper hurried out the back door. The early-afternoon spring sun shone down on the new pale grass sprouting up through the dried brown remnants of last year's yard. A slight breeze blew, enough to cool the air, but not leave things chilly.

She ran through the weedy yard, past the gazebo and

what had been a vegetable garden, to the tall blue spruce trees bordering Grandma's yard. Slipping between two trees, she came out to discover a small dirt path running between a fence and the trees. She'd run straight to the developments behind Grandma's house.

Looking wildly around, Piper didn't see any black holes in the yards or fences, so that much was all right. But she also didn't see the path she usually took to get to Larkingtower's spire. Not so good. Squelching her panic, she retraced her steps to the house. She could still get to Fairy. She'd just forgotten to concentrate on where she was going before she left the house.

Entering the kitchen, she saw the small stone mead jug sitting on the counter, surrounded by the remnants of her hasty breakfast and the other things from the basket Malraux had given her. A momentary impulse seized her to drink some of the thick sweet mead—she'd need all the energy she could get—but she ignored it. Concentrating on getting to Aelvarim, she left the house again. This time the yard was greener, less weedy, the development was gone, and the familiar dirt path wound over the leaf-strewn ground, between thick evergreen trees, up and down over rolling hills.

The increasing number, and size, of the black holes scared Piper more than she could say. She dodged around them as she hurried past, taking note of where they lay on the ground around the path, in case she had to leave the path to get home again.

A thin tendril of smoke rose from the top of Larkingtower's stone spire, but Piper just hurried past, running swiftly over the rolling green meadow. She hurdled the stream and kept going into the forest on the other side at a dead run, leaping over gaps in the path, dodging when she couldn't leap. Panting and gasping for breath as she ran.

The glade by Malraux's cavern was coated in black

splotches. The contrast between Malraux's home and
Larkingtower's struck her, as she turned down the path
to Aelvarim's house. If the gaps started first in the areas
of Human and Fairy farthest apart, then Malraux was
much farther from human influences than Larkingtower.
Piper wondered how that might have affected his relationship with Grandmother Dickerson.

She nearly flew across the tree-bridge to Aelvarim's
house. The shimmer was gone, but the house remained.
It was a quaint stone cottage, one door, two windows,
steep roof, and flower beds across the front. It too gave
Piper the same strong impression of a face as Grandmother's house did. She knocked, but Aelvarim didn't
answer.

Malraux did.

"Come in," he said, opening the door wide. "Aelvarim
isn't here, but I expect him back soon."

She looked around without stepping in. Inside was a
single room. A large fireplace with a roaring fire domi-
nated the far wall, giving the inside of the cottage a
heavy smoke scent. A few pieces of rough furniture and
a few pots and pans completed the decorations. On a
heavy wooden table sat the statue Malraux had been
carving. Piper could see now that it was someone mining
with a pick.

"Thank you, but I really need to find Aelvarim.
Quickly."

"What seems to be the trouble? May I help?"

Try as she might Piper couldn't make the laugh lines
around his small dark eyes into sinister crow's-feet, and
his beard-covered, rosy, chubby cheeks looked more
Santa-like than dastardly evil. In person it was hard to
imagine him casting a murder spell on anyone.

While she hesitated on the doorstep, Malraux stepped
out of the cottage, coaxing gently, "I know Aelvarim
was upset about something this morning, but he

wouldn't say what. Please, let me help you."

Piper gushed in panicked worry, "There are gaps appearing in the Human realm. I don't know what to do. I need to talk to Aelvarim and find out if he's found out anything more to add to what we discovered last night." She found she was wringing her hands.

"Oh." Malraux appeared flabbergasted and worried. "Time is running out. Aelvarim said he was going to look for clues in the Human world. You might find him there."

"But where there? Do you know where he might be?"

"I don't know. I've never been to the Human world. I'm sorry, but I don't know."

"The gaps, in the Human world, I was the only one that could see them. How can people avoid them if they can't see them? Is Aelvarim safe there?"

"No one is safe anywhere now." Malraux wrung his hands. "People in the Human world can only see the gaps if they know about the world of Fairy. You can see the gaps because you know what used to be there. You've been tainted enough by Fairy that you still remember. For everyone else all that no longer exists, and never did. You'd better hurry; find Aelvarim. If gaps are appearing in the Human world also, there isn't much time left. The rift will continue to grow, until our worlds are ripped apart and there's nothing left. Hurry." He waved her off.

Piper ran back the way she'd come, through the darkening forest. It wasn't until she'd reached Larkingtower's spire, and stepped out into the meadow, that she realized it wasn't night coming on, but the gaps swallowing up the sunlight trickling through the forest's leaves and branches that were making it appear dark.

A trail of smoke from the chimney of Larkingtower's spire let her know that he was at home, but she didn't want to disturb him. She wasn't sure if he'd assist her, shout at her, or just ignore her, if she were to stop and ask.

She continued at a normal pace across the meadow, to allow herself to catch her breath and give Larking-tower an opportunity to step out and offer to help her if he wished. But the door to his spire remained closed, and she heard no sound from within.

The forest path back to Grandma's house was dappled with shadow and black splotches. Some of the trees drooped; even the evergreens seemed gray and foreboding. No flowers raised their colorful heads to cheer her. Spring seemed blighted with a return of winter, even though the air was still warm, and beyond the forest the sun still shone down. The real and illusory ability of the gaps to swallow the light withered the beauty of the forest.

Entering the house, Piper looked around. Somewhere around here there were clues, or at least a clue, something to let them know what had happened to Grandma. Who had tried to cast an evil spell that was now ruining both worlds? And what had that person done?

Piper concentrated on finding Grandma's manuscript. The fairies' dream returned to her, starting with her opening the trunk in the attic, pulling out the wedding dress. . . . She stopped herself; this was no time for foolish fairy shenanigans.

She hadn't checked the wardrobe yet. She raced into the bedroom and started flinging her things from the wardrobe onto the bed, careless of any damage she might be doing to the antique wooden wardrobe. When she'd cleaned out Grandma's clothes, she hadn't thought to look for hidden drawers or such. Running her fingers along the bottom, back, and sides produced no secrets, no hidden drawers, no splinters. Under the crumbling paper lining of one drawer she found a picture.

Sitting in the window seat, Piper examined the old,

faded picture. It was her great-grandparents' wedding picture. Grandma was wearing the wedding dress from the trunk up in the attic. Grandpa was looking nervous in his suit. Something seemed wrong to Piper.

Grandpa's arm was down by his side. He had no black book in a white-knuckled grip in his hand.

That had been in her dream. So her dream image had differed from reality. That was no big surprise. But the book had been in more of her dream than just in the picture. Where? Piper remembered the book had been at the bottom of the trunk with the wedding dress. So what?

"The book is in the bottom of the trunk!" she shouted at herself. The fairies had been trying to help her, and she hadn't paid any attention. She needed to apologize to them. If she ever saw them again.

Her attempt to fly up the narrow stairs to the attic failed, and left her crawling swiftly up with a bruised knee. She fumbled with the lid to the trunk, and it squealed in protest as she opened it.

The smell of mothballs rose from the trunk as Piper disturbed the contents. She carefully removed the wedding dress, keeping it still in its rustling paper wrapping, setting it gently on the stack of trunks. The paper-wrapped veil followed it. Then Grandpa's suit.

At the bottom of the trunk, along with a layer of crumbling old mothballs, was a stack of yellow, legal-size pads, with a faint scrawling script covering them.

Piper snatched the stack of legal pads up and started to leave. She set them down to replace the suit and veil and dress, and to close the trunk. The clothes had lasted this long, it would be a shame to lose them because of her carelessness.

She raced down to the kitchen to read the handwritten manuscript. She didn't have time to read thoroughly, she skimmed the pages, looking to catch the gist of the story, and hoping not to miss any clues.

The faint scrawling script was difficult to make out, and the yellow paper didn't help any. There were cross-throughs and notes going chaotically up and down in the margins. All the splotches, blotches, misspellings, and mistakes that had always made handwritten documents so tedious were flagrantly displayed on the yellow pages.

Slowly she read, occasionally skipping whole passages or pages, rarely turning back to catch something she missed.

It was a story of a human woman. Piper couldn't find any clear reference to the woman's age. Sometimes the woman seemed to be an older woman, sometimes a younger woman. Even knowing the author had been a great-grandmother was no help in determining the age of the character. After all, Grandma had at one time been a young woman.

In the story the woman has been dabbling in magic, and, through her attempts to learn and cast spells, accidentally stumbles onto Fairy. She attempts to learn the ways of Fairy to help with her magical undertakings. However, she quickly becomes caught up in how the worlds of Fairy and Human interact with each other. How they affect each other. And how they provide wonder to each other.

She meets several denizens of Fairy, but only the fairies were well-defined. For most of the other characters it was difficult to determine what species or sex they were. Though Piper couldn't be sure whether that was due to the author's inability to clearly define her characters, or due to the current reader's careless skipping of certain passages in her haste to finish the manuscript.

As the story progressed, the woman was assisted in her discoveries by an undefined male figure from Fairy. He provided her with spell books, assisted her research, gave her pointers, and generally was nearly obnoxiously helpful.

It was plain that he loved her, but that she was interested in him only as a friend. She felt it would be impossible to ever love him, since she didn't fit in his world, and he didn't fit in hers.

Piper picked up the last yellow legal pad, now reading every faintly scrawled word.

The story had reached a confrontation between the woman and her male friend. He declared his undying love, offering her his heart and everything that he had, if only she would be his. He was determined to prove that he was her one and only true love, and that nothing could ever keep them apart. That there was no impediment that was insurmountable, no chasm of differences too great to span. There was nothing, absolutely nothing, he wouldn't do for her.

She tried ever so gently to explain how much she valued him as a friend, but only as a friend. He wouldn't listen. When the heroine declared her final no, he went crazy, throwing spells like a two-year-old in a tantrum. When that didn't change the heroine's mind, he begged and pleaded, clutching her arm.

Then he threatened to kill himself, or her, or both of them. To bind their souls together. If necessary to destroy both worlds to keep her with him.

Piper flipped the last page up, to confront the plain, unmarked cardboard backing to the legal pad. There was no more story. The ending was missing.

She searched back through all the other legal pads, but she'd looked at all the previous pages. The ending wasn't there. She looked a second time, then a third.

Each pad was numbered, at the right corner of the upper binding, and on the reverse side of the cardboard backing. Each page was numbered, bottom center, sequentially from the first, so that even if one or more pages had come loose from the others, they could still be put back in order.

Had she left one in the attic? Piper retraced her steps, carefully checking the floor and stairs. No more yellow legal pads. She opened the squealing lid of the trunk, carelessly lifted out the dress, veil, and suit. But only broken and crumbling mothballs covered the bottom of the trunk.

With care she put the clothes back in the trunk and closed the lid. Back in the kitchen she searched again through the stack of yellow legal pads.

The story had no ending.

Had Grandma not gotten to the ending? Was this what Aelvarim meant when he said they had to complete the story? Or had Grandma tucked the end in another hiding spot, to keep it safe from whoever was trying to destroy her?

Piper flipped back through the pages but could glean nothing more from the story. Mostly because she was skimming it even faster than the first time, while she thought.

Aelvarim had said that the manuscript would hold clues to who had murdered Grandma. Piper didn't see any clues there that she hadn't come up with by herself already. It had to have been someone Grandma knew in the world of Fairy: Aelvarim, Malraux, or Larkingtower.

Larkingtower pretended to hate women, but secretly liked them. He'd saved Piper from attack by the fairies, then run her off with his spells. He'd been trying to do what he could to stop the rift. That was really all Piper knew about him.

Malraux seemed so nice and kind. He'd given Piper the stone to keep the fairies away, shared his mead, and welcomed her into his home. But, he hadn't lifted a finger to help Aelvarim solve this puzzle, other than offering a bit of advice.

Aelvarim was handsome enough to catch any woman's interest and leave her drooling, even Grandma. He was the only one of the three that Piper could imagine showing that kind of willingness to help, offering his assistance in learning and research, or giving out spell books.

She stopped herself, reviewing that train of thought. The logic was inescapable. Piper rechecked a few passages in the manuscript, making sure she hadn't misread the faint scrawling script.

It had to be Aelvarim.

Piper looked up from the manuscript. Aelvarim was standing in the open kitchen doorway, watching her.

FIFTEEN

"IS IT?" AELVARIM ASKED HESITANTLY,
looking hungrily at the stack of yellow legal pads.

Piper felt her heart and stomach sink. Before she
could think of anything to say, Aelvarim swiftly crossed
the kitchen to sit in his chair at the table. He took the
pages from her with the care due a rare religious artifact
and began to read at an extraordinary rate. While he was
turning pages nearly as fast as she had been when skimming, Piper had the impression that he was reading
every word.

A glance out the window showed that the sun had just
set. Piper got up, inching away from him, and turned on
the kitchen light. The better to see what she was doing.
"I'll just fix us something to eat."

She remembered the first morning she'd found him in
the kitchen and the fear she'd felt. Wondering who he
was and what he was doing there. Piper wished she
could adequately compare her feelings, then and now.
She still wondered who he was and what he was doing.
She was still afraid of him. But, was she more afraid

then, when she hadn't the slightest idea who or what he was, or now, when she'd learned just enough about him to know she didn't know him? And now that she feared she knew what he'd done.

Peanut butter and jelly sandwiches would give her an excuse to get a knife out of one of the drawers. She could secretly slip a sharp knife into her pocket, to defend herself if need be. If only she had bothered to find the knives since she'd first met him.

Putting the peanut butter and bread down on the counter, Piper glanced over at Aelvarim. He appeared to be absorbed in his reading, head down, face close to the pages, staring intently. Piper opened the new jar of peanut butter, unable to really savor the strong just-opened peanut butter smell.

Now was the time to get the knife. Maybe she'd get lucky, and he wouldn't notice. Piper closed her eyes, concentrating on locating the sharp knives with the spell he'd taught her. Going straight to the correct drawer, she opened it to find a jumble of utensils; spoons, forks, egg beaters, serving tongs, instruments of unknown usefulness and provenance, spatulas, and knives, sharp and dull.

Risking a glance at Aelvarim, Piper palmed a sharp all-purpose knife, just larger than a steak knife. She slid it, point-end first into the front right-hand pocket of her pants. With her other hand she withdrew a dull knife to spread the peanut butter. Aelvarim never looked up from Grandma's manuscript. Hopefully, he didn't suspect a thing.

Trying for casual, and fearing she looked nervous, Piper spread peanut butter on two slices of bread. When she leaned down to get the jelly from the lower shelf in the refrigerator, she heard a faint rip and felt the knife point nick her leg. Standing she could feel the cool blade of the knife, quickly warming, sliding alongside her thigh below the bottom of the pocket. She had to get the knife out and find a better hiding place for it.

Slipping her hand, oh so casually, into her pocket, Piper accidentally pushed the hilt of the knife through the tear. Leaving her holding nothing but pocket lint. The knife came to rest just above her knee.

Abandoning any hope of using the knife to defend herself, Piper switched to hoping she didn't hurt herself on it before she could get it out of her pant leg, with Aelvarim none the wiser.

She finished the sandwiches and put one in front of Aelvarim. He picked it up automatically and took a bite, without noticing Piper's stiff walk, or even, as well as Piper could tell, what he was eating.

Piper leaned against the counter to eat. She couldn't sit for fear bending her leg would cause the knife to cut into her knee. Stripping out of her pants there in the kitchen wasn't an option; Aelvarim would be bound to notice that. The bathroom was too far away for her to walk to without the knife slipping or slicing.

Aelvarim picked up the last pad of paper.

Perhaps with a little surreptitious wriggling of the leg she could coax the blasted thing to slide down to her ankle without cutting anything en route. She could ease it out onto the floor and kick it somewhere Aelvarim wouldn't see it, but where it would be handy for her to grab, just in case.

The knife slipped and caught, slipped and caught, as she wriggled her leg. Aelvarim remained head down in the last pages of the manuscript, apparently oblivious to her delicate squirming problem. Piper could feel the perspiration gather on her as she struggled to finish getting the knife out before he finished the manuscript.

A small clattering clink was all the knife made as it slipped out of her pant leg, over her shoe, and onto the floor. It was enough. Aelvarim had just turned the last pad of paper over looking for the ending. He turned to face the noise, setting the last pad gently on the stack with the others.

He looked from the knife, lying inappropriately on the kitchen floor, to Piper, who knew her face showed her guilt and fear, to the unfinished manuscript stacked neatly on the table beside his half-eaten sandwich. Aelvarim's gaze went around from the knife, to Piper, to the manuscript a second time.

Flinging his arms in a wide sweep across the table, Aelvarim scattered peanut butter sandwich, plate, manuscript, and miscellaneous papers across the kitchen floor. The plate rolled to a ringing stop as he put his head down on the table, cradled in his arms, and began to weep.

Piper's feelings ran the confused and confusing gamut from guilt to pity to annoyance. Crying wasn't going to help anything. It certainly wouldn't clean the mess he'd made all over the kitchen floor. Which, Piper knew, in the end would be left for her to do something with.

However, she did know exactly how he felt. She almost wanted to join him, put her own head down, and cry. The hopelessness of the situation, with gaps showing up in the bookstore, and her own feelings of helpless inadequacy, she'd determinedly suppressed. He looked so pitiful.

Her foot kicked the knife as she started to walk to him.

"I would never hurt Grandmother Dickerson," Aelvarim managed to choke out around his sobs. "I wouldn't hurt anyone. What a monstrous cruelty to think that I would."

She stooped to pick up the knife.

His head lifted slightly from his encircling arms on the table, and she paused, but he didn't see her holding the knife. His eyes were filled with tears, and in any case, he was looking at the table.

"The manuscript was my last hope to find whoever murdered Grandmother Dickerson." He paused to gulp down a sob and push the tears around his face with his hands. "Now that hope is gone. I can find no clues in the story to reveal who the villain truly was. If there are clues, they are beyond my comprehension."

The knife clinked and rattled amongst the other utensils, when Piper dropped it in the drawer. Poor Aelvarim. She wondered if it was just him, or if all elves were this sensitive. Looking at him now, the thought that he might try to murder Grandma was ridiculous.

Aelvarim wiped the tears from his reddened face but remained staring at the tabletop. "It has to be here, in this world, probably in this house. I haven't found any clues anywhere else. And yet . . ." He spread his hand out to the manuscript pages on the floor.

Piper walked over to stand next to him.

"I'm sorry," he whispered.

She patted his shoulder. "It's all right."

Suddenly Aelvarim stood, wrapping his arms around her, pulling her close to him. He hesitated a moment, then his head descended and his mouth met hers.

His arms around her were warm and strong, his kiss sweet. Piper never felt happier or more content. She put her arms around his waist and held on for dear life.

It was a few moments before they came up gasping for air, before she could make herself think of anything beyond what she felt. As Aelvarim pulled her close a second time, a little nagging doubt crept into her thoughts.

He'd put spells on her before. Was this another?

Piper pushed away from him. Aelvarim loosened his grasp but kept his arms around her. He looked down at her puzzled.

"Have you cast a spell over me?"

"No." He watched her face a moment. "Do you doubt me?"

"You lied to me."

Aelvarim let go of her and stepped away, as if she'd burned him. "I've never lied to you."

"You asked me to read the labels on the bottles to you, telling me you didn't understand them, but you read the books without a problem."

"There's a difference between 'Once upon a time' and 'Lemon Scented Scotch Pine Ammonia,' " he said scornfully. "The words 'Lemon Scented Scotch Pine Ammonia' held no meaning for me. Which is why I asked you to explain them."

"They don't make any sense."

"My point exactly."

"Nothing was labeled 'Lemon Scented Scotch Pine Ammonia.' Those words in that order are ridiculous," Piper shouted.

"I don't remember what they were labeled," Aelvarim shouted back. "But none of them made any sense to me, so I had you explain it so I could take them to Larkingtower."

"And what did he say?"

"He said they were female paraphernalia." Aelvarim frowned fiercely, trying to hide a blush. "And that I should get rid of them, immediately."

After a moment's consideration of Larkingtower's multiple failings, Piper muttered, "He would."

Aelvarim stepped close to her, running his hand up the back of her arm. "I've never lied to you, and I wouldn't cast a spell like that on you. I would never hurt you."

"I have to think," Piper whispered. It was hard to think with him so near, so warm and cuddly.

"I love you." Aelvarim took both her hands in his,

clasping them tightly. "I love you now and forever, with an unchanging, undying, unbounded love."

Piper looked up at him in surprise.

"There's nothing I wouldn't give if you would be mine. I have only my own, unworthy self to offer, but that I give you freely. My heart, my hand, my eternal devotion, all that is mine to command, I give to you. I realize you consider us a mismatch, parted by our different worlds. . . ."

How could he know?

"Regardless, you are my one and only true love, and I am yours. Nothing can keep us apart, if love joins our hearts and minds. As our worlds meet on this hallowed spot, we, too, can carve out a place for us to meet. There is no insurmountable impediment that we cannot overcome, no chasm of differences we cannot span. . . ."

Wait a minute.

"There is nothing, absolutely nothing, I wouldn't do for you. Please accept my love and allow me to prove that we are meant to be." He lifted her hands to his lips to kiss them. "My love, allow me to make you happy."

Pulling her hands out of his grasp, Piper backed away from him, slipping on a stray piece of paper on the floor. "That was almost verbatim from Grandma's manuscript!"

"It's true!" Aelvarim stepped toward her.

"Does that mean you are the one that murdered Grandma? You had that speech down cold. Did you give her a similar speech?"

"No!" Aelvarim recoiled, horrified. "Grandmother Dickerson? Never! I loved her dearly, but not . . . No!"

"So why did you use that speech?" Piper carefully stepped around one of the manuscript pads, pushing it toward the counter with her foot.

"I can't help it." Aelvarim still looked horrified.

"Oh, please! Don't tell me you can't help it." Piper

leaned over to open the utensil drawer without taking her eyes off him. "You most certainly can help it." Her hand fumbled through the contents of the drawer, searching for a handle with the feel and texture she remembered from the knife.

Aelvarim shook his open hands in frustration. "I told you Fairy is influenced by stories. I can't help it."

"So you are the man in that story." Piper's fingers closed in on a familiar handle, and she grasped it, pulling it out and thrusting it toward Aelvarim.

They both looked at the egg whip she was pointing at him.

Pulling himself up straight and dignified, Aelvarim said calmly, "May I point out that you are behaving exactly like the woman in the story. Does that make you her?" Piper refused to answer. Aelvarim continued, "I'm no more the man in that story than you are the woman. That is merely coincidence."

"Then why the speech?" Piper shook the egg whip at him. It might not be a knife, but she'd bet it would leave a few marks if she hit him hard enough.

He frowned, and drew a deep breath that threatened the seams of his skintight tunic. "I have had some very strong feelings for you. That I ought not to have acted on. I apologize. It was not my intention to injure you or in any way threaten you."

"Ha!" She had him this time. "You've used spells on me before." She shook the egg whip again. "The first morning we met you cast a spell on me."

"You wanted to throw me out! You weren't going to listen to me otherwise," Aelvarim said. "I had no choice."

"I'll throw you out now!" Piper screamed.

She lunged at him with the egg whip. Throwing his hands up defensively, Aelvarim ducked out of her way. She slashed at him again, and he retreated from her. All of her blows whistled through the air, missing their target, but she managed to back him up against the kitchen counter. He leaned back on the counter to avoid being hit in the face.

"Stop that!"

"All right." Piper leaned over him, grabbing him by the lacings on his tunic front. She intended to haul him by them to the door, but the warm smooth touch of his skin on her fingers distracted her. She closed the minuscule distance between them and kissed him.

Aelvarim tensed, then relaxed almost to the point of melting on the counter. He wrapped his arms around her. Piper kept hold of his tunic front, but when she went to put her other hand around his neck, she smacked the side of his head with the egg whip.

"Ouch."

"Sorry."

He took the egg whip from her and threw it across the room. Piper heard it hit the far wall with a strange sound, a sort of combination thump and crack. Her fingers worked their way into the silky strands of his hair. She ran one fingertip up the side of his ear, touched the point, and kissed him again.

Only a desperate need to breathe again made Piper surrender the kiss. He looked at her longingly; his hand caressed her hair. "I think I shall die if you say you won't be mine."

Piper jumped away from him. "Stop that! Quit quoting the manuscript. It's creepy."

"I apologize. I don't know what else to say."

"Don't quote, just say what you really think. When you quote it sounds like you're lying."

Aelvarim looked around the room, obviously at a loss. He looked everywhere but at Piper.

"You are the one from the manuscript." Piper's voice shook, nearly as much as her hands. Her heart pounded with misery and frustration. "You killed my great-grandmother." Piper opened the utensils drawer again.

"No. I swear it. I never harmed Grandmother Dickerson." Aelvarim dashed for the back door.

"Get out! You lying, murdering . . ."

He flung the door open wide, and paused in the doorway looking back at Piper. "I love you. I want to marry you."

"Get out!" Piper grabbed a handful of utensils and threw them at him. "I hate you!"

The door slammed shut, as the utensils skittered across the floor without reaching the door. Tears clouded Piper's eyes, her throat constricted around her breathing, and she gasped, trying not to sob.

SIXTEEN

PIPER WALKED AROUND THE KITCHEN, STOOP-
ing often to pick up papers, manuscript, sandwich, plate, and various utensils spread and smeared across the kitchen floor. The sandwich she threw in the trash, the plate and utensils were tossed in the sink. The papers and manuscript she placed on the table.

Wiping her hot salty tears away, Piper sat at the battered kitchen table and began reordering the yellow pads of manuscript paper, making sure all of them were there, with all the pages still attached, in good shape, and in proper order. She couldn't help reading the last section over again, the fight. As best she could tell, nearly everything Aelvarim had said to her was from the manuscript.

Though his actions had been different. In the manuscript the characters hadn't kissed at all. Nor had the woman character chased the male around with an ordinary kitchen utensil. And the male character never specifically told the woman he wanted to marry her, just that he wanted her to be his.

Reading it now, it seemed more of a threat than an

endearment. As if he wanted to possess and control the woman, not marry her. His pleadings somehow twisted in this new light into arrogant commands, his pretty words vicious threats, and his tactics coercive. Piper could only assume that either she or Aelvarim had misinterpreted the manuscript. Or both.

Piper carefully stacked the yellow pads, with the first pages on top and the last on the bottom. She stared at the thin, faint, scrawling script, willing the manuscript and her dead grandmother to help her in some way. Nothing occurred to her. She pushed the stack away from her, sighing. Regretting her own confused and hasty actions and words to Aelvarim, she looked up at the back door, wondering how far he'd run when he left so hastily.

Next to it a black hole gaped in the wall.

Her chair fell backwards, landing with an echoing thud on the kitchen floor. Piper barely caught herself before she fell with it. A hole in the wall? A rift here in Grandma's house? Already?

Fear and fascination drew her unwillingly but inexorably toward the gaping black rip in the wall. As she cautiously approached she noticed pieces of ripped, faded wallpaper hanging down into the hole.

It wasn't a rift. Someone, or something, had punched a hole in the wall.

Still she gingerly extended one finger hesitantly to probe the tattered edges of the wallpaper. The paper gave under her fingertip, and she didn't disappear. It was just a hole punched into the wall. She picked a hanging shred of faded wallpaper, fluttering near the top of the hole, and pulled. A roughly triangular fragment ripped away from the wall.

Piper could see where the drywall ended, in an almost-straight horizontal cut. She'd thought the whole house had been built in the days of plaster. Had this wall at some point been rebuilt using drywall instead?

Pulling away other bits of wallpaper revealed a nearly square hole in the drywall, a handspan in height, encompassing the entire width between two wall studs. Someone had cut a hole into the wall, and then wallpapered over it to cover it up.

Why cut a hole in the wall, and then paper it up? The only reason Piper could think of was to hide important items. A clue? Probably not. After all, how had Grandma found the time after she'd been stricken, but before she went to the hospital. This hole had to predate Grandma's illness. Unless Grandma had anticipated problems and prepared for them. That would be like the Grandmother Dickerson Piper remembered.

Piper could almost see something lurking in the dark shadowy recesses of the hole, a gleam of metal. Hesitantly, she reached inside.

Her fingers touched the familiar cold metal loops of an egg whip. Laughing at herself, she boldly reached in, grasping the egg whip by the jointure of the loops and the handle, to pull it out. The backs of her fingers brushed against something cardboard, leaning up against the outside wall of the hole, as she pulled the egg whip out. Something else in the hole? She threw the egg whip on the floor and carefully put her hand in the hole again. Piper easily found the cardboard, grasped it, and pulled it out.

It was a legal-size pad of yellow paper, with a faint scrawling script covering it. Numbered on the upper right hand binding and on the back, with page numbers at the bottom of each page. The numbers taking up where the others left off. It could only be the end of the manuscript.

She rushed to sit at the table and began reading.

This writing was fainter still than all the others, and so scribbled and scrawled that it was difficult to make out, as if written hastily by someone that wasn't at all sure of what they were writing. Piper read slowly and carefully. Here would be the clues she needed.

This portion of the manuscript clearly defined all the characters that had been so nebulous before. It identified the vague male figure from Fairy, who had so harassed the heroine in the previous installments, as a wizard. The heroine was a young widow, still mourning her recently dead husband. The reason she could never love the wizard was because she would always love her deceased husband, the real true love of her life.

The wizard couldn't, and wouldn't, accept this. He didn't appear to be all that sane on any count. He threatened now not to kill himself or the heroine, but to throw a spell over her. He said he would bind her soul to him, to Fairy, away from her dead husband's, even if it threatened the very worlds of Fairy and Human.

The heroine stalled for time, knowing she didn't have the necessary power and knowledge to combat his spells. She escaped his wrath by pleading with him, and was given three days in which to reconcile herself to her fate. She retreated to her home, preparing what simple protective spells she could to aid herself.

She called upon her sister for assistance. The sister was apparently, unknowingly, a very strong but untried sorceress. The two of them also went to a friendly young elf for help. While not as powerful a mage as the wizard, the elf had in his favor his youth, honor, and a raw genius for magic.

While spying on the woman, the wizard found out about the three conspiring against him. Before they could mass their powers against him, he bound the sister and the elf hand and foot with his spells. Leaving the woman to face him alone.

Attempting to fend off his spells, the woman couldn't concentrate well enough to launch an attack of her own against him. She barely managed to keep up her own defenses. The elf and the sister combined forces to break the wizard's bindings. This distracted him enough that the woman was able to bring up her strongest defensive spell, a mirror spell, while he re-bound the sister and the elf.

When the wizard launched his next attack, it was mirrored back on himself. Without any defenses—he didn't expect to need them against her—he was incinerated by his own spell.

Piper flipped the page, to find cardboard.

The end? No wrap-up, no denouement? This was one story where Piper wanted to see the "And they all lived happily ever after" part. Especially since it wasn't really done yet. At least it wasn't finished yet for her. It would be nice to know now that it all turned out all right in the end. No such assurance there.

But clues, yes, she finally had the puzzle pieces all in place. It was so obvious now. Why hadn't Grandma made it obvious in the other manuscript.

Because it was Larkingtower. And Larkingtower, with his spell-casting ability, might be able to ferret it out and destroy or obliterate the manuscript. Or perhaps he'd cast a spell that wouldn't let Grandma put it down so plainly on paper, and she'd only managed to get the truth buried and coded in this way on the one yellow pad with the very faint, extremely scrawled, laborious handwriting.

Larkingtower was the only one of the three males in Fairy close enough to the juncture with Grandma's house having enough knowledge of spells to be able to do that. Larkingtower hated and despised women, while simultaneously hiding a passion for them. Serious insanity, that. And the gaps were supposed to show up first in those places between the two worlds that were least connected. Larkingtower obviously had more contact with the Human world, and Grandma, than the other two. How could Malraux cast a spell on someone in the Human world if he'd never been to the Human world?

Which made Piper's earlier suspicions about Malraux seem ridiculous. Luckily, she'd only shared them with Aelvarim. She felt incredibly guilty about suspecting Aelvarim. Worse, she'd confronted him about it. Accused him to his face of murdering an innocent old woman he cherished. Remorse and shame over her conduct burned through Piper.

How had they missed the obvious clues pointing to Larkingtower? The exploding spell in the garage. Only Larkingtower could have done that. Grandma didn't have the knowledge, Malraux never entered the Human world, and Aelvarim admitted he didn't have that kind of spell-casting power. Larkingtower had tried to convince them it was only paint. How could paint break and char a broom?

Had he needed the broom and the pot holder for his spell? Something, or several somethings, that were personal items belonging to his victim to complete his odious spell. What else had he used, that Piper was even now ignorant of? And what was his spell?

Piper flipped back through the last pages. A binding spell—in the manuscript the wizard threatened to use a spell to bind the woman's soul to him and to Fairy. Had Larkingtower bound Grandma Dickerson's soul to him and to Fairy? Was that what was causing the two worlds to pull apart? From what Piper could recall of spells, a natural recoil against an abnormal binding might in fact be the cause of the rifts.

Unable to remember any particular binding spells, Piper hurried to the parlor and pulled Grandma's spell books from the shelves. There weren't any spells that purported to bind souls, but there were several petty binding spells. One that supposedly made regular glue into a superglue, but after a moment's distraction on that spell, Piper returned to searching through the spell books for spells to bind souls.

Few counterspells were listed. Most seemed to involve the destruction of something particular to the binding, generally through burning it to ashes. Unfortunately, Piper didn't know of any burnable thing that might particularly pertain to this binding. And in any case, there was more involved in even the simplest of binding counterspells than just the burning of an object.

Returning to the kitchen, Piper reread the final section of the manuscript, looking for clues to counteract a binding spell. The part where the sister and elf unbound themselves to fight the wizard was terribly uninstructive.

Larkingtower would know. Piper wondered momentarily about the advisability of just walking up to his door and asking. With both worlds about to destroy themselves, could things really get any worse?

Would Aelvarim know?

There was only one way to find out. Piper dreaded confronting Aelvarim, after some of the things she'd said and done. Could he forgive her for flinging the contents of the utensils drawer at him?

How had he missed all the clues that they'd run across? He'd been spending his time looking for clues and not seeing any.

Of course, he hadn't wanted to believe that it had to be one of his friends and mentors. Aelvarim had naturally shied away from the thought that the people he knew, and admired, and were so precious to him, had committed so heinous an act. Piper couldn't blame him for that.

After all, her only excuse for not figuring things out earlier was stupidity. She'd at least had the advantage of being an outsider looking at the whole situation from a different angle. She should have seen, she should have noticed, she should have known.

Method, motive, opportunity, all pointed to Larkingtower.

Knowing she had to find Aelvarim and let him read the final installment of Grandma's manuscript, and that delaying was only making things worse, Piper picked up the last yellow legal pad and clutched it to her.

She took a moment to try to find the words to say to Aelvarim. "I'm sorry" seemed inadequate, but she didn't have time for a long-winded explanation. Maybe she could just give him the pages to read. After they'd figured a way to defeat Larkingtower, released Grandma, and saved their worlds, he'd forgive her.

Barring that, she could always try kissing him again. He seemed to like that. It couldn't hurt.

Pushing her chair back, Piper resolutely stood up. She was tired and worn, physically and emotionally, from her fight with Aelvarim. Anticipating a long night's work, Piper walked to the counter and uncorked Malraux's mead. She took a swallow and recorked the jug, waiting for the sweet thick mead to work.

With the jug in one hand and the final section of the manuscript in the other, Piper approached the back door.

"I need to get to Aelvarim, in the world of Fairy, as quickly as possible."

Keeping her concentration on her goal, Piper stepped outside into the dark.

SEVENTEEN

IT TOOK A MOMENT FOR HER EYES TO ADJUST TO
the dark night outdoors. A little rectangle of light spilled
from the kitchen window. Using the outlines of the light
on the grass as a guide, Piper made her way quickly to
the gazebo. It stood a strong, tall, solid gray shadow
against the dark backdrop of the blue spruce trees. Once
beyond the gazebo, she negotiated by moonlight, past
the borderline of trees, and into the forests of Fairy beyond.

The gaping black rifts had increased, dappling the
path, and merging into strange Rorschach spots, making
running along the path impossible. Piper picked her way
carefully and as swiftly as she could through the quiet
dappled shadows of the moonlight forest. There was no
sound other than her footsteps, and her heartbeat
drummed loudly in her ears.

To get to Aelvarim she would have to pass Larkingtower's spire and the worst of the rifts' gaps around
Malraux's cave. She planned to give Larkingtower's
spire a wide berth. She didn't want to run into him to-

night. Malraux's cave might be more difficult, depending on how thick the gaps were. She wasn't sure if Malraux's grove and cave might not be gone, vanished into an enormous rift.

If that were so, it was possible that Aelvarim might not have made it home on the path past Malraux's cave. In that case Piper wasn't sure where she'd find him. He'd never spoken of another path to his house. She feared he would stay with Larkingtower, and wondered what to do if it looked like he couldn't have made it home. She decided to worry about that later.

The path ahead was riddled with gaps. Piper walked off into the darkness under the trees and discovered that while there were more shadows and less moonlight, there were fewer gaps out beyond the path. It didn't make sense, but she took to running through the trees away from the path, trying to keep an eye on where the path wandered as she went. By treating the path as a directional guide and making her way through the forest, she was able to make better time.

What would she do after she found Aelvarim? How could they defeat Larkingtower? The first part of the manuscript had been vague enough that she could see either herself or her great-grandmother in the woman's role, in fact any woman could have fit into the role. Unfortunately, any of the three male denizens of Fairy of her acquaintance could fit the male role in its vague state. Did the fact that the final portions of the manuscript dictated certain roles for certain people mean that Piper couldn't fill the role of sister? She wanted to worry about that later, but couldn't.

Grandma Dickerson never had a sister. Surely she wouldn't have written it that way if it had to be a sister. Surely any female relative would do. Piper hoped.

In that case did the fact that the wizard in the manuscript had been defeated mean that Piper needn't worry,

Larkingtower's defeat was certain? She doubted that. If she could substitute as sister, Larkingtower could figure a way out of his demise.

Piper didn't know any spells or counterspells in any case. Maybe it was hopeless. Maybe she should just leave it to Aelvarim to solve.

Yes! He'd said he was a storysmith. He's asked her to help him find the murderer and finish the story. She didn't have to do this all by herself. She'd found the explosion in the garage, found the manuscript, found all the clues in fact. Once she'd turned the manuscript ending over to him, they would have found the murderer, and he could tell her what they had to do to finish the story.

If only she could find Aelvarim.

The locate spell would work. It might even work better here in Fairy than it did in the Human world. Maybe this wouldn't be as difficult as she thought. Piper hoped.

She paused a good way back from the opening to the meadow around Larkingtower's spire. The meadow beyond the forest seemed to glow a strange, ultragreen in the bright light of the nearly full moon. She could see each little hillock, outlined against its neighbor. From this far back on the path she was at the wrong angle to see the door of the spire, but she could see the stones, caressed by moonlight, looking solid and hard. The spire and the strange light lent an eerie malignity to the bright pastoral meadow. A thin stream of smoke curled across the face of the moon from the chimney on Larkingtower's spire. He was home.

Piper concentrated intently, trying to locate Aelvarim. She hoped so much and so hard that he wasn't with Larkingtower, that her first attempt failed. She silenced her hopes and fears, faced Larkingtower's spire, and concentrated on finding Aelvarim in this world.

Not in the direction of the tower, that feeling came to

Piper strongly. She slowly turned, all the way around, then kept turning past facing the spire to a stop where she felt the strongest that she was facing toward him. She might have been able to put a compass point to that direction during the day if there weren't clouds blocking the sun and she had some time to figure it out. In the night she had no idea which way she faced, no idea what sort of terrain lay between her and her goal, and no idea where that direction might lead her.

Other than it would clearly lead her the long way around Larkingtower's meadow, to get back to the path she knew by the brook. She opted to go the short way around to the path she knew.

Trying to move silently, Piper tiptoed around twigs and leaves unsuccessfully. The pines had dropped their thin needles in a thick coat over the floor of the forest. Every step she took crackled. Piper hoped she crackled silently, and hoped Larkingtower was sound asleep in his bed.

She reached the dried-up streambed. A river of black now coated the area where the brook once trickled. Only this river didn't flow. It lay still, an inky black malevolence flooding the defeated banks of the vanquished stream.

As Piper looked up and down the banks for a good crossing place, she felt vines quickly twine themselves around her ankles. She experienced a moment's irritation, remembering the last time the fairies had pulled this trick on her. Then she grinned, at least the fairies were back.

"Figwort," Piper called, slightly above a whisper. "Where are you? I don't have time for this. I need to find . . ."

"Aelvarim?" Larkingtower asked, walking out of the shadow of a tree. His long bony finger pointed at her.

The stone mead jug and yellow legal pad were pulled

from her hands. Something tugged at her, and she fell forward, onto her face on a bed of pine needles. Vines grew up her to twist around her arms, fastening her wrists together.

"Malraux's not-so-secret vice," Larkingtower sneered as he negligently tossed the mead jug into the black stream. A feral smile winked across his face as he watched it disappear. He turned his attention to the pad of paper. "And Alfreida Dickerson's foolish ramblings. She had no talent for stories at all, you know." He sighed. "This one never was of any use for her purposes."

"Give that back!" Piper screamed. She struggled against the vines, only to discover they grew and thickened the more she struggled. They grew up her legs and arms, wrapping themselves around her body tighter and tighter, until she felt them become snug around her chest. She lay still, and they stopped growing further. "It's not yours."

"You weren't of any use either." Larkingtower flipped a few pages and sniffed scornfully. "This ending will never do."

"Give that back!" Piper hated the whiny screech to her scream. "You can't do this."

"But I can. Silly girl. They say never send a boy to do a man's job. And I had always thought that referred to Aelvarim. But this is even more pathetic, sending a girl to do a man's job." Larkingtower flipped the pad over to look at the back. "Where is the rest?" he asked mildly.

"Safe from you," Piper snarled back, trying to hide her fear not only from him but from herself.

"False bravado. I'll find them. You probably just left them sitting out on the kitchen table. Very careless of you." Larkingtower shook his head. "You were so pitifully obvious. I once considered directing you to Aelvarim as he took his bath in the river around his moat, but thought that would be unfair to him. And I always wondered what would happen if I told you"—he leaned down to whisper—"he does his laundry in a teacup, since the clothes he wears are elf spelled to fit, and thus actually doll-sized." He stood and nodded, more to himself than Piper. "Yes, indeed, your eyes did bulge out of your head. I thought so. Pitiful."

Flipping a few more pages, pausing here and there, Larkingtower appeared to actually read portions of the manuscript, ignoring Piper. She thought furiously, unable to do anything else. He suddenly laughed at something and smoothed the pages back down over the cardboard.

"Alfreida might have been a doddering old fool, but she had better sense than you. However, I like your stubborn sense of determination. It will come in handy for my purposes once I've bound you to my service." He grinned at her. "Bending your will to my spells will be so exhilarating. I hadn't realized until I bound Alfreida, the joy to be found in the unbreakable control of a contrary spirit. Watch. Maybe you'll learn something."

Larkingtower tossed the pad of paper into the air. The pages splayed and flapped as the pad flipped and twirled. Larkingtower shouted a single syllable, and the paper burst into flames.

"No!" Piper screamed, making the word last through several agonizing seconds.

The burning pad of paper fell to the ground, becoming a pile of ashes as it hit.

A trail of dusty smoke rose from the ashes, curling and weaving, thickening and spreading. It took on a shape, vague at first, then focusing into that of a woman, old and stooped. The bottom of the smoke trail broke off from the manuscript, and the smoke woman floated up, away from the pile of ashes, to hover over Piper.

Piper felt strength flowing out of her and into the ghost.

"No," Larkingtower said in a commanding voice. "Stop. Now. Heed me."

"Yes!" Piper shouted, putting all her will behind pushing her strength into the floating form. Anything that Larkingtower didn't want, Piper wanted, badly.

The smoke took on a more solid form as she watched, but remained translucent. It settled into the image of Grandma Dickerson.

"Piper. Are you all right, dear?" she asked in a ghostly quavering voice.

"I forbid this," Larkingtower commanded.

"Tisk, tisk." Grandma shook her head at him. "Who cares?"

"You are still bound to me." Larkingtower motioned at the ghost, as if to pull it toward him.

"No," Piper shouted. Her fingers wiggled, and she pulled back, concentrating as hard as she could.

The shade of Grandma Dickerson floated, teetering between them, as if pulled in a tug-of-war. "You destroyed part of the manuscript that I wrote and that Piper owned. You know the consequences of that sort of thing. I'm now only partially bound. I told you you'd never get away with this."

Grandma sounded calm and certain. It only served to make Larkingtower madder. Smoke curled from the edges of his robe and from the length of his beard. His twisted, bony fingers curled and uncurled, demonstrating his anger and frustration, and his knuckles cracked loudly.

Piper whispered, "I don't think he's working with a full spell book, Grandma. I don't think you should be taunting him. This is not the time."

"Hush now," Grandma said, shaking one ghostly finger at Piper. "I lived a good deal longer than you, and

I've been dead longer than you. I know what I'm doing. As long as we work together everything will be fine."

A shout from Larkingtower in a strange language thundered through the forest around them and echoed from the meadow behind them. Grandma's shade was pushed back, past Piper, partially dissipating, then coalescing back together. The trees shook, and a wind stirred the dust and needle bed of leaves Piper lay on. She closed her eyes and turned her head to keep the sharp, pointed pine needles and stinging sand out of her face.

"Enough." Larkingtower raised his arms high above his head. The loose sleeves of his robes fell back to his shoulders, revealing stringy gnarled arms, mottled from the smoke rising around him in the moonlight. A wind stirred the hem of his robes and the trailing strands of his beard, but it didn't reach his hair or sleeves. "You want to be together? I'll bind you both. Now."

Shadows and smoke gathered between his hands, like clouds massing for a mighty storm. His voice rolled and stirred the mixture, with words that Piper not only heard, but felt. Electricity sparked from his fingertips into the cloud between his hands, highlighting it in a momentary flash of lightning. His hands moved farther and farther apart to span the growing mass. His feet spread, and his back bowed under the weight he held.

Piper screamed, an inarticulate longing for help. If only she'd found Aelvarim first.

EIGHTEEN

A GOB OF THICK GRITTY MUD HIT LARKING-
tower square on the face, splattering into his eyes and
wide-open mouth, effectively silencing his thunderous
chant. He choked and sputtered. His contorted hands released the roiling storm of cloud and electricity above
his head, and the clouds of his spell began swiftly dissipating and losing energy. Larkingtower spat mud and
bracken from his mouth, while his gnarled, bony hands
wiped the mud from his eyes.

Piper tried turning her head to see who had thrown
the mud missile, but the vines held her tight. She looked
up at Grandma's hovering ghost. "Who is it?"

"Aelvarim." Grandma's ghost appeared to crouch, to
whisper to Piper. "Remember what I said, we must work
together, with Aelvarim. Only by joining our strengths
can we succeed."

"Feminine matrices?" Piper said, incredulously.

"Not necessarily feminine," Grandma chided. "Wasn't
it Benjamin Franklin who said, 'We must all hang together, or assuredly we shall all hang separately.' "

Out of the corner of her eye, Piper saw Aelvarim moving carefully around the black rifts by the dead brook, making his way to the opposite side of Larking-tower. He was frowning as he risked a quick glance at her. He strummed his harp, and the vines around Piper loosened. She pulled her arms out of the shrinking vines, and started to get up.

"I think not," Larkingtower shouted. He pointed a long bony finger at Aelvarim. A ball of fire bloomed from his fingertip, arcing toward Aelvarim.

Changing the tune on his harp, Aelvarim couldn't stop the fire ball from hitting his chest, but did manage to avoid being burned or singed. He flipped and rolled such that he didn't land on any gaping rifts.

Piper's arms were free, but she was still caught in the vines, kneeling. Grandma's ghost drifted off, in the opposite direction from Aelvarim. Piper realized they'd end up at three points around Larkingtower. The electricity of his spell seemed to have expanded, Piper could feel goose bumps on her arms and legs. The meadow and forest crackled with energy, leaving a strange, acrid, metallic taste in Piper's mouth.

"Give up!" Larkingtower shouted. "The three of you combined don't have the power to stop me."

Looking to her comrades as they slowly moved into position, Piper hoped they had a plan, or at least knew how to defeat Larkingtower. While the three of them might outnumber Larkingtower, and have him surrounded, Piper wasn't sure exactly what she, personally, could do against him.

Maybe she could distract him with really cutting remarks. She wished she'd paid better attention to the spell books.

A movement far away caught her attention. She hoped it might be someone coming to help them, maybe Malraux. Instead, she saw the gaps at the farthest edges of her sight growing, by slow inches, true, but still fast enough to be noticeable if watched.

Larkingtower launched a few more fireballs at Aelvarim, who danced and dodged around the rifts surrounding him like a minefield. Grandma, having reached a point about midway around Larkingtower from both Aelvarim and Piper, extended her hands toward Larkingtower.

Grandma moved her hands and fingers up and down, as if raking him from head to toe. Larkingtower shuddered and turned to face Grandma's shade.

"Begone," he commanded, flicking his hand in her direction to dispel her. Grandma began drifting off, and pulled herself back with a look of determination.

Aelvarim stroked a chord on his harp, making a pulling motion with his other hand.

It looked as if some unseen hand had pulled on Larkingtower's long, gray, wispy hair, jerking his head back, nearly pulling him off his feet.

Quickly glancing from Aelvarim to Grandma, with his back to Piper, Larkingtower launched two fireballs at his adversaries, simultaneously. Aelvarim and Grandma both dodged. The smell of smoking green leaves shot through the charged battleground.

Piper truly wished she'd paid better attention to the spell books. She could have used a really lethal spell. She could remember the titles of a few spells, but they weren't the sort to hurt someone with. All she knew for certain, that she could use, was the location spell. Unfortunately, she already knew the location of her worst problem. She wished she could relocate him.

Or locate something she could use to fight him.

While the others exchanged spells, Piper concentrated hard, looking around her, at the forest and meadow. What could she use to fight Larkingtower?

The cold stone spire held much promise, but with the

unbreakable vines holding her fast, she couldn't reach anything that far away.

She could use the mud, dirt, and leaves surrounding her, if she could form them into a missile to throw at him. She didn't dare attempt it. Tiny new pale green vines sprouted around her, waving up at her from the ground, as they tried to reach her arms and hands to bind her. Sticks and stones presented the same problems.

The trees themselves might be fashioned into any number of weapons depending on the type of wood: pine, maple, or oak. In fact, there didn't seem to be anything around her that couldn't be used against Larkingtower, if only Piper were free to forge weapons from them.

The manuscript. The ashes of the manuscript lay in a small pile not far, and yet too far, from where Piper knelt. Piper felt most strongly that even though ashes, the manuscript was the most potent weapon they had against Larkingtower. She couldn't reach them.

Looking up, she saw Larkingtower lob another volley at Aelvarim and Grandma. Grandma's shade looked paler. Aelvarim appeared singed, with charred spots across his tight tunic and smoke rising from his scorched hair. Both looked weary.

Risking the waving, eager vines, Piper attempted to snatch up a small brown stone off to her right. With their master busy elsewhere, the little vines weren't fast enough, and Piper's fingers closed on the cold rock, lifting it up from the leaf-littered ground. She took aim, and threw.

The rock hit Larkingtower's robe-covered back, just after Grandma raked him, but before Aelvarim pulled his hair. Piper feared that his layers of robes, and the distance, might have cushioned the blow.

Larkingtower spun around and kept turning. He held his gnarled hands out straight from his shoulders. His robes swirled and spun out around him like a cone from his waist down. A powerful wind circled the meadow and the forest. Piper was somewhat sheltered by the surrounding trees, but Aelvarim and Grandma's ghost were out in the open meadow.

Grandma began to dissipate, spreading out over the wind. Aelvarim was too busy dodging flung-up debris from the forest, sticks and twigs and pine needles and leaves, and avoiding rift holes, to fight Larkingtower effectively.

The ashes of Grandma's manuscript lay in a quiet pile on the ground, undisturbed by the whirlwind, as if holding themselves together against whatever Larkingtower might throw at them.

"The manuscript," Piper shouted, glad that the wind was circling toward Aelvarim from her, and so might help carry her voice to him. She wasn't sure how much he'd seen and heard before he'd started his attack against Larkingtower, and added, "The ashes! They're a weapon."

Aelvarim nodded. Piper could see him stroking his harp, but she could hear no music from it. He made slow progress into the buffeting wind, trying to dodge the flying debris and the growing black holes made by the rift.

The far-distant horizon was now completely black, as if nothing existed beyond this battleground. Piper could see the gaps around them growing now. Slowly, slowly, but again noticeable if she watched.

Piper tried to get another rock. This time a small tendril of vine looped itself around her elbow. She flung the stone at Larkingtower, managing only a glancing blow against his moving outstretched hand, before the vine expanded and tightened around her arm, pulling her hand to the ground.

Grandma threw a little ephemeral cloud at Larkingtower. Aelvarim shouted something, and punched one tightly balled fist toward Larkingtower. The cloud settled itself in front of Larkingtower's face, and his knees bent suddenly, pitching him down, like a tree falling.

Larkingtower twisted as he fell. He launched another fireball at Aelvarim. The cloud swirled down to block Larkingtower's face as he hit the ground. Aelvarim and Grandma launched new attacks as Larkingtower's gnarled fingers hooked the cloud with arcane twists and smeared it against the ground.

Piper struggled against the vines pulling her toward the ground. Now would be a good time to whip a knife out of her pocket, or even a rip in her pants, but unfortunately she hadn't thought to try putting one in her pocket before she left. Considering the luck she'd had the last time she'd tried putting a knife in her pocket, it probably wouldn't have worked.

A fireball streaked across the meadow, highlighting the green rolling hills slowly being swallowed by gaping black splotches. Aelvarim dodged the spell, and it charred an innocuous patch of grass near the bridge. One of those fireball spells would fry the vines that bound her.

How to get Larkingtower to fire one at her?

If the location spell worked by concentration and an act of will, maybe other spells worked the same way. Piper stared at Larkingtower. He was facing her way, so she couldn't see much of his hair, but she had a fine view of his frowning distorted features and dangling wind-whipped beard. Thinking hard, she imagined reaching out and pulling on those long, wispy strands of gray hanging down past his knees.

Larkingtower's head bobbed.

Shouting incoherently, he pointed his knobby finger at her. A spot of fire blossomed from the tip of his finger, growing and spreading as it neared her.

Searing heat hit her, washed over her in a deluge of scorching flame. Her skin sizzled, and her hair crackled. Smoke flowed over and around her, coating her with a gritty layer of inky sticky ash. She was thrown forcibly backwards. Thick moving vines tightened, ripping at her, only to flare up with momentary flame, turning to charred tattoos flaking off her arms and clothes.

From her vantage point—lying on her back on the forest floor, staring up at the bright uncaring stars in the black velvet of the night, with smoke rising in lazy coils from her and the dried leaves around her—she realized that perhaps this wasn't the best of all possible ways of getting rid of the vines binding her.

She coughed the cloying smoke out of her blistered lungs, past the searing pain in her throat and the gummy coating of rancid soot in her mouth. With a supreme effort she pulled herself up to a sitting position. Cinders fell from her hair onto her face, and she rubbed the stinging grit from her watering eyes.

From the sounds of wind and fire, the battle still raged. Clearing her sight of soot and tears, she found that Aelvarim had nearly worked his way to the ashes of the manuscript. Grandma was hovering on almost the opposite side of Larkingtower from them, and so faded that it was hard to make her out against the backdrop of the meadow and trees. Only the growing black gaps provided enough contrast with her waning form to allow Piper to see her.

With blind desperation, Piper jumped to her feet, charging Larkingtower, yelling at the top of her lungs.

Larkingtower pointed his finger at her. She ducked below the crackling fire. Her shoulder hit Larkingtower just above his belt, her arms wrapped around him tightly, and she tackled him to the ground.

A strong vicious push caught her in the ribs. She flew back, through the air, hitting her back up against a tree

at the edge of the forest. She slid down, feeling small
branches snap beneath her and the rough bark rip at her
shirt. Her back and ribs ached from the pummeling, but
the remaining smoke had been cleared out of her. Piper
gasped for breath, forcing the air into her unwilling
lungs.

"May I?" Aelvarim asked from nearby, where he
crouched beside the small pile of ashes that had been
Grandma's manuscript. His hand hovered above the pile,
hesitantly.

May I? May I what? Unable to speak yet, Piper nodded. Sure, whatever you want.

Aelvarim hummed, and stroked his harp with his left
hand, while scooping up a handful of ashes with the
right. He sprinkled the ashes into the nearest gap, rubbing his fingers to clean them of any lingering bits.

The gap was growing at a much faster pace than any
Piper had seen before. She looked around her in horror.
The widening gaps had grown to dominate the land-
scape, leaving a few shrinking islands of green forest
and meadow. As she watched, the islands grew smaller
and smaller.

Larkingtower screamed, a high-pitched sound of pain,
and launched himself across the expanding black gaps
to grapple with Aelvarim. Aelvarim managed to sweep
another handful into the gap before Larkingtower
grasped him.

Pulling herself painfully away from a growing black
rift on her right, Piper barely had time to rejoice that
they'd finally found something that could cause Larkingtower some real pain and problems.

Strain and fear marred Aelvarim's face as Larkingtower pulled Aelvarim's hand away from the harp. Fire
and smoke billowed up from where Larkingtower's
hands had grasped Aelvarim's arms. Grimacing in pain,

Aelvarim kicked the last of the ashes into the gap. Larkingtower screeched.

Piper pulled her knees and feet up to her, making herself as small as she possibly could. She had to keep herself in the shrinking island of forest around her. Grandma floated over to hover, nearly beyond sight, above Piper.

Aelvarim dropped suddenly, bending his knees and landing on his back, pulling Larkingtower over with him. He flipped Larkingtower over with his feet, to land in a large, black, gaping rift.

Howling, Larkingtower slowly sank into the gaping rift, his grasp tightening on Aelvarim's arms. Aelvarim pulled against the sucking tow of the black maw. Struggling and twisting with all his might, he tried frantically to break Larkingtower's grip on his arms. With a bleak, despairing look at Piper, he vanished into the rift.

Piper tried to stand, but the ground shifted beneath her, and she pitched forward, toward the blackness surrounding her.

NINETEEN

PAINFULLY BRILLIANT LIGHT WOKE PIPER.
She blinked the light of the rising sun out of her eyes,
pushing herself into a sitting position, half-leaning
against the rough bark of the pine tree next to her. She
rubbed the sleep from her eyes, brushed the dead pine
needles off her arm, and tried to finger comb needles
out of her snarled hair.

"Good morning, Piper," Grandma said.

Grandma sat on a little hillock not far away, just up
from the arched wooden bridge. Her dark old-lady eyes
stared piercingly at Piper from her wrinkled, pale face.
Her nearly white hair gleamed in the sunshine, and her
hunched shoulders leaned toward Piper. In her pale dress
she appeared fragile and indistinct.

The newly risen sun blazed in a soft, clear blue sky.
The grass under Grandma was a bright springtime green.
A bit of a chill, either lingering from the night or due
to the season, hung in the air. The crystal-clear brook
burbled along in its bed of rounded pebbles.

"Am I dead?" Piper asked.

"No, dear, I'm dead." Grandma floated upward, so that Piper could see that she was more or less transparent. "You're very much alive still."

"Larkingtower!" Piper stood abruptly, making her head swim. "Aelvarim! Where are they?"

"Gone. I'm afraid."

Off in the meadow, Piper saw the ruins of an old stone tower. Portions of the once-proud chimney had fallen, to pile up in the tall neglected grass and weeds around the sagging spire. Rocks lay on the ground around the tower where they'd fallen, leaving shadowy holes like lace in the wall of the spire. The door stood half-open, stuck and warped and skewed and rotted.

"Gone where?" Piper leaned against the tree, holding tight to the rough bark of a branch to keep herself upright. "What happened to Larkingtower's spire?"

"What we did last night . . . changed everything. Larkingtower is gone, and Aelvarim with him." Grandma looked off at the ruins decorating the meadow. "We've never had much luck with wizards in that tower. Though usually they only self-destruct. The first one I knew was a youngish fellow, for a wizard, named Mendevrak. He was constantly experimenting, the absentminded scientist sort, until he did himself in." Grandma's ghost floated over closer to Piper. "The second one was Septery—an egotistical, pompous idiot—who attempted to change the fabric of Fairy himself." Grandma shook her head sadly. "Larkingtower, you met."

"But what of Aelvarim?" Piper asked.

"Last I saw, he was pulled into a rift, into nothingness. He doesn't exist anymore."

"You mean he's dead?"

"No, dear," Grandma said. "You can only be dead if you were alive at some point. Aelvarim was swallowed by a rift. He doesn't exist. He never existed. That's what happens to things and people in a rift; they're gone, completely."

"And Malraux?"

"I wouldn't know, dear. Perhaps he's fine."

"Maybe he can help us." Piper hurried off over the arched wooden bridge and down the path through the morning-dappled forest. The bright springtime greenness had returned to the forest, and the gaps were completely missing. Piper noticed her rumpled clothes were still smudged and singed from the battle, but they were merely stained, with no noticeable odor of smoke or filth.

From back at the meadow, Grandma called, "Malraux help us? Help us how? The danger is past. It's over."

"Aelvarim." Piper continued down the worn path through the trees. "I'm glad Larkingtower is gone, but we have to get Aelvarim back somehow."

Grandma appeared suddenly, floating on the path ahead of Piper. "Why is that, dear?"

"Because he didn't do anything wrong. Because he didn't deserve that. Because I never had a chance to apologize."

Piper crossed over the familiar stone bridge and walked into Malraux's grove. Tall weeds and thorny bramble filled the rocky grove, concealing the entrance to the cave, forcing Piper to struggle past, adding rips to her rumpled, stained clothing, and scratches on her sore arms and legs. The cave entrance was where she remembered it being, dark and breathing cold air out of its maw. However, there were no cheerful, welcoming carvings on the plain, weathered rock.

Using her hands to guide her through the stygian darkness in the cave, Piper slowly and bumpily worked her way through the two one-eighty turns, and stepped into a cold, echoing, empty blackness. A faint eerie light grew back in the tunnel behind Piper. Grandma's ghost floated in, providing an unearthly light that displayed the dark shadows of the cavern and highlighted the more sinister aspects of the shadowy stalactites and stalagmites.

Nothing remained of Malraux's home. The enormous fireplace, carved-stone furniture, wooden table and benches, sawed-off stalagmite niches, were all gone. Or rather appeared never to have been at all.

"Where is he?" Piper asked sadly, her voice echoing in the recesses of the cavern. "What happened to him."

Grandma's ghost bobbed up and down, moving slowly around Piper. "I was afraid of this. Whenever changes come from outside of Fairy, owing to, say, a change in stories or some such thing, the change is easy and they all remember it. No harm done. But whenever someone from Fairy tries to institute a change from their side, through any means other than the influence of human imagination, catastrophic things happen. In this case, Fairy seems to have lost at least three of its denizens. I'm afraid all we have left of them may be our memories."

Piper's hand reached for the talisman, hanging on a chain under her shirt. It was still there. Piper pulled it out of her shirt. "Look, see here is the rock Malraux gave me, which I dug from his mine. Aelvarim charmed it to keep the fairies from pestering me. They did exist. We have more proof than just our memories. They were here, they're not now, and I'm going to get them back, somehow."

"Whatever you say, dear." Grandma's ghost smiled in the darkness as it bobbed around the stalagmites.

Groped her way blindly, Piper made it through to the opening passage out of the cave. She couldn't stop herself from walking to Aelvarim's house. She wasn't sure if she just wanted to prove to herself that he wasn't there or if she actually hoped against hope that he was. The path remained, and the hollowed-out fallen tree bridge was still unchanged, as were the cliffs and the quick stream circling the hill. The house, however, was gone. Nothing left.

Standing on the opposite side of the fallen tree-bridge, Piper realized how much she'd hoped for something, anything, to be here. Some sign that Aelvarim had existed, or that she could somehow change things so that he would exist again. She resolutely crossed the bridge, determined to find some crumb, some speck of proof to show that she hadn't made all this up in her mind.

And now who was crazy?

Ignoring her own thought, Piper started up the green grass-and-weed-covered hill. Halfway up, she noticed what she thought was a faint shimmer at the summit. She ran up, to find a small stone carving resting on a large flat rock, surrounded by sweet-scented flowering weeds.

Malraux's carving. The one that looked like someone driving a pickax into a large outcrop of rock. It shimmered at the edges. Piper knelt to get a better look at it. The miner appeared to be Malraux, complete with beard and leather apron. As she watched the figure stretched and lengthened, morphing into a very good likeness of herself, in her regular blue jeans and shirt, with no beard, of course. After a moment it continued, lengthening until it became Aelvarim, tight tunic and leggings stretched taut to cover him. She watched as it cycled back to Malraux.

Slowly and carefully she reached for the shimmering statue, grasping it tightly with both hands around its wide base. It wasn't as heavy as Piper had expected it to be. She pulled it against her, to steady it and assure herself she wouldn't drop it.

"Well, dear, that's strange. I've never seen anything like it before." Grandma floated beside her. "It's very nice, though. Malraux always was very good at that sort of thing."

Piper walked back home, carefully clutching the statue to her the whole way. She set it down finally on the table in the center of the parlor.

"Quite a job you've done in here, dear," Grandma said as she looked around the parlor while floating into a chair. "I was beginning to worry that no one could ever get this house straightened out. Well done."

According to the clock, it was almost nine o'clock. Knowing they would expect her soon, Piper called Independent Books, to tell them she wouldn't be in. Mavis answered, and accepted Piper's excuse of illness easily.

When she returned to the parlor, Piper found Grandma still sitting in the chair, watching in rapt fascination as the shimmering statue went through its changes.

"Incredible. Isn't it?" Grandma said.

"Yes. It's very nice." Piper leaned wearily against a full bookshelf. She felt battered and bruised, tired and depleted, dirty and grubby. And now she had a ghost to tend to, along with the house and all her other problems. "Do you think any of these spell books could help?"

"Help what, dear?"

"Aelvarim."

"I don't know. I was never all that good at actually performing spells. I just thought they were interesting." Grandma began thinning, fading, as she sat primly on the chair. "Why worry about him? He was only an elf. They're a dime a dozen in Fairy. I've been through three wizards so far. I'm sure another elf will show up to take Aelvarim's place." While Piper watched, she became transparent, disappearing completely.

Maybe Grandma was right, Piper thought as she headed for the tiny cramped bathroom to get a much-needed shower. Afterward, she collapsed on top of the soft covers of her bed and slept.

The roaring growl of the vacuum sweeper woke her near noon. Piper stumbled unwillingly out of her soft warm bed, rubbing the sleep grit from her eyes. Her clothes clung in sleep-ironed wrinkles to her. She pulled and smoothed her clothes into something resembling comfort. Who would be vacuuming the parlor of Grandma's house?

Grandma.

Piper blinked at the vacuum sweeper, apparently pushing itself merrily across the empty carpeted floor. The chairs, table, lounge, and conversational were all sitting quietly on the front porch, like bad children lined up to be given a stern talking to.

"What are you doing?" Piper asked the air.

"I'm vacuuming, dear. You've been working so hard, I thought I'd help you out." Grandma's ghost faded in, to where Piper could see her pushing the vacuum. "There's so much to do here. Too much for one person."

Back in her warm, soft bed, Piper wondered about her own sanity, but not enough to prevent her from falling asleep again. The brisk slapping sound of a wet mop striking the kitchen floor woke her next. Piper pulled her pillow over her head. The pillow couldn't block the rattling of pots and pans in the kitchen, but Piper persevered, remaining in bed and trying to relax.

"Piper!"

Realizing she'd been asleep, Piper got up and wandered out to the parlor again. "What now?"

Africa and Sherlock stood hesitantly just inside the open doorway. Sherlock held a towel-wrapped casserole dish. Africa looked around the parlor in wide-eyed wonder.

"Aunt Nellie said you'd called in sick to work, so I knew our dinner date for tonight was off, but we wanted to come by and bring you something." Africa's blonde hair bobbed gently as she nodded to the casserole dish.

"Did you just call in sick so you could clean?"

"No. Grandma did that," Piper said without thinking.

"Grandma?" Africa asked.

"She's a ghost. She wanted to clean. I was tired." Piper looked around. The old parlor had been vacuumed and dusted to within an inch of its life. The wood of the chairs gleamed, and the room smelled of lemon oil.

"And the elf?" Sherlock sounded concerned. "Is he still coming to dinner."

Piper knew Sherlock had always seen her as an island of sanity in her eccentric family. Piper hated to think he'd changed his mind about her.

"No. He's . . ." Piper thought furiously, "left the country." Sherlock only looked slightly relieved. "And he's not . . . I mean, he's one of the neighbors. Was one of the neighbors."

Africa motioned for Sherlock to take the casserole into the kitchen. He started forward, and she followed behind nearly pushing him. "Well. I'm sorry we won't get to meet him. We just wanted to leave this for you. It's too bad you were feeling ill today. The relatives had their business lunch today, and you missed it. Aunt Nellie was peeved. She says you'll never get the hang of it if you don't show up."

In the newly cleaned kitchen Sherlock set the casserole on the stove and took his babbling wife by the hand. "We'd better be going. Piper isn't feeling well and needs her rest."

He herded Africa out, while Piper smiled gratefully at him and waved good-bye to them both.

The kitchen had been thoroughly scrubbed and polished. The floor shone as if waiting for a commercial to be filmed. The countertop stood proudly immaculate and bare. Piper wondered where all the papers and such had gone. Probably the cupboards. The sink and chrome fixtures sparkled. Pine essence and lemon oil thickly scented the air. At least Grandma hadn't used bleach.

Under the towels the casserole was still warm. It was a savory ham-and-potato casserole, a well-known family recipe. The wonderful smell wafted up, and Piper discovered she wasn't tired anymore. She ate in silence, waiting for Grandma's ghost to show up. After doing the dishes, she called out, "Grandma!"

No answer.

"Underfoot all day. Going through the house like a one-woman cleaning tornado. Making enough noise to rouse the dead. Then you can't find her when you need her."

Puttering through the four small rooms of the house took no time at all. Piper didn't find Grandma in any of them. She thought about walking through the yard, maybe checking the gazebo and garage, but she couldn't face the thought of leaving the house. If she left, would she find Fairy? Was it even there anymore? The thought of finding only the dreary Human world was depressing.

There was still a lot of cleaning to be done in the house. Piper needed to dust and vacuum the bedroom and scrub the bathroom. Not that she expected she could do as good a job as Grandma. In any case, neither of those options sounded all that exciting.

Piper headed for the attic. She wasn't sure exactly what she would do up there, but at least she could rationalize avoiding the other work by claiming to be working in the attic. At least, to herself.

Everything was as she remembered it, large dark trunks stacked neatly, junk piled everywhere. She lifted the squeaking lid of the trunk with Grandma's wedding dress, to check that everything had been put away neatly. It looked more hastily put away than neatly.

She pulled out the dress, gently unwrapping it from its paper. The dress had yellowed with age, but that only made it look exactly like it did in the aged photograph.

She carefully rewrapped it. Then she removed and rewrapped both the veil and Grandpa's suit.

As she put the suit back in the trunk, she felt the bottom board in the trunk shift under the suit. The trunk itself hadn't moved, just the bottom board. Taking the suit back out, Piper looked into the trunk.

The bottom appeared to be a thick piece of cardboard, skewed higher at one corner and lower at the opposite. Piper grabbed the corner of the cardboard and pulled it out. Underneath was a yellow legal pad covered in a faintly scrawled script.

She pulled the legal pad out and hastily returned the false bottom, suit, veil, and dress. The lid almost didn't have time to creak as she slammed it down.

In the kitchen Piper read the new ending to the story. This ending had only a few things in common with the ending destroyed by Larkingtower. The only real similarity was that the characters were well-defined. Other than that, this ending was completely different. This version had no wizard.

The male from Fairy was a handsome elf, and the heroine a young unmarried woman. The elf regretted his threats, but continued his declarations of love. To prove his sincerity, he assisted her in finding and casting the spell she needed to fix a wrong in the Human world.

Due to the peculiarities in casting this spell, the woman realized that the only way she can truly know and understand the world of Fairy and all the wonder in the Human world, the only way she can perfect her spell-casting abilities and become her most true ultimate self, is to fall in love with Fairy. She must fall in love with the world of Fairy, the essence of Fairy, and its representative, the elf.

In this version, all ended happily.

Piper wished she'd found this version before she found the other. Though it wouldn't have helped solve the mystery of what had happened to Grandma.

Reading it again, she was struck by how like Aelvarim the elf was, patient, tenacious, and just a little foolish. Of course, Grandma undoubtedly had Aelvarim in mind when she'd written this ending.

And the manuscript confirmed another suspicion Piper'd had originally. Grandma couldn't have helped trying to play matchmaker with her great-granddaughter and that handsome elf. Even if only in her dreams.

Smiling, Piper set the manuscript aside.

"So, do you like it?" Grandma hovered anxiously by the back door.

TWENTY

"CAN'T READ ANYTHING IN THIS HOUSE,"
Piper muttered.

"What, dear? I don't understand."

"It's very good." Piper put it on the bottom of the stack of manuscript pads. "Yes, I like it."

"Thank you, dear. It's very nice to hear that." Grandma floated over to sit opposite Piper at the table.

"Would you mind if I typed it up, and submitted it to publishers?" Piper asked.

"Do you think it's that good?" Grandma's ghost looked surprised. "Do you think they'd publish it?"

"I liked it." Piper shrugged. "The only way to find out if they'd publish it is to submit it."

"That would be so wonderful." Grandma looked dreamy, one hand on her cheek, supporting her head as it leaned to the side. "I always wanted to write a book, and then buy it at the bookstore. I bought so many books over the years." Grandma sat up straight. "Connlan, your great-grandfather, used to laugh, and say that it was a good thing I was born when women were allowed to read; otherwise, I'd have been nothing but trouble." She smiled. "I think he enjoyed having a wife that loved books as much as he did. He bought as many as I did. We used to love to share them and discuss them. Even when we disagreed."

"Grandma, I don't want to be rude, or hurt your feelings or anything, but I wondered . . ." Piper groped for the right words to say. "Now that you're . . . dead, aren't you supposed to go on . . . to wherever? Go to the light or something?"

Looking sad, Grandma said, "Yes. Connlan has been waiting for me for such a long time now, and I for him."

"So, why are you waiting?"

"Well, dear, I'm stuck. Things are not as they should be. As Aelvarim would say, you have to fix the story."

"I have to fix the story? Why me?"

"I'm dead, dear. What can I do?"

How to answer that? Piper sat back in her chair. "So what do I have to do to fix things?"

Grandma floated up off the chair. "I don't know. I was never very good at casting spells or figuring these things out. Aelvarim was very polite about it, but it was obvious I was hopeless." Grandma floated over to plant a preternatural kiss on Piper's head. "You'll do fine, dear. You solved my murder, didn't you?"

"Not very well! I made this whole mess."

"You'll do fine." Grandma faded completely away.

"Your faith in me is touching." Piper pushed away from the table, scraping her chair on the shiny floor. She picked up the computer. "Someone in this house is touched." She gently placed the computer on the table-top and slammed herself back into the hard kitchen chair. "Touched in the head."

Picking up the first yellow legal pad, Piper started typing the manuscript into the computer. She made a few changes as she typed, fixing obvious typos and grammar problems, and defining the characters from the beginning.

AT INDEPENDENT BOOKS THE NEXT MORN-ing, Mr. Gumble glanced up from the register as Piper walked in. "You look like you're better. How are you?"

"Much better. Ready to go back to work." Piper tried to appear more energetic than she felt after staying up half the night typing. The bright sunshine, and the combined book and coffee odor of the store, helped.

Mr. Gumble didn't look convinced, but he nodded anyway. "Take it easy today. You've got the register."

The day passed slowly. Piper ran the register, and straightened and reshelved. About midafternoon Mavis wandered up to the register, looking at the rumpled, scribbled-on pages of her inventory printout rather than where she was walking.

"I'm sorry, Piper." Mavis spread the print out on the counter beside the register. "It was right here all the time."

"What?"

"*The Power of Imagination, from Fairy Tales to Philosophy.*" Mavis pointed to a line of type on the printout, with a handwritten number one next to it. "It's right here on the printout like you said. And there's one copy on the shelves. I'm not sure how I missed it. I thought you'd messed up because you were coming down sick. Sorry."

"Oh well." Piper reminded herself to breathe. "As long as the inventory is all straightened out in the end. That's all right."

"Don't know how I could have missed it." Mavis shook her head and flipped through a few pages in her printout coming back to the same entry.

"Computer glitch probably," Piper volunteered. "If I recall correctly it wasn't on the screen."

"Hmm." Frowning, Mavis wandered back to the office while flipping through her printout.

Sometime later Piper saw Mavis and Mr. Gumble conferring over the rumpled pages. Mavis was still frowning. Mr. Gumble looked only vaguely annoyed and kept shrugging at what Mavis said to him.

Piper did some quick checking before she left work. Both *Power of Imagination* and *Feminine Matrices* were on the shelves. She wondered if this meant that there were no changes in the Human world because of what happened in Fairy.

SHE TYPED ALL EVENING, WITH ONLY A short pause for dinner, but still didn't manage to get the manuscript completely entered into her computer. Grandma didn't show up, or say boo. Though at one point Piper called to her to help interpret a particularly squiggly scrawling passage that seemed to have more cross-outs, blotches, and misspellings than any other.

HARM—DRESSED IN A RED-LEATHER MINI-skirt, white-ruffled shirt, and enough gold-and-silver baubles to start up a small business—greeted her the next morning with a cheery, "Good to see you back. We missed you."

"Good to be back," Piper said.

As it was Saturday, customers swarmed the store, keeping the employees bustling. Piper kept busy restocking shelves and finding books for customers. Using the simple location spell, if the store had it, she could find it. Even if it was hiding in the used-book annex. She rapidly gained a reputation for knowing the stock, which impressed even Mr. Gumble.

Just before the end of their workday, Harm pulled Piper to the side to ask, "So are you going out with your boyfriend tonight? Would he be stopping by to pick you up, maybe?"

"What boyfriend?" Piper asked, while automatically straightening the shelf in front of her.

"The incredibly handsome one. Aelvarim." Harm looked at Piper like she was dense. "Surely you remember him."

"Oh. Yes. I mean no. I mean, yes, I remember him, but no, we aren't going out tonight."

"Too bad." Harm sighed, and reached to straighten a high shelf. She winked at Piper. "Though if you two are on the outs, maybe I can catch him on the rebound."

"Not this time."

Harm shrugged. "Well, I really just wanted another opportunity to drool over him from afar."

"I'll see if he can stop by another time."

PIPER SPENT ANOTHER EVENING TYPING the manuscript into the computer. The next day she had off work, and finished the manuscript before lunch. She still hadn't heard from or seen Grandma. After lunch Piper searched the house and yard, without finding Grandma.

She stepped into the house and looked around the parlor. The parlor was clean, with a lingering trace scent of lemon oil, there was only the bedroom and bathroom left to clean in the house. Piper felt an urgent need to go search for Grandma in Fairy. It certainly beat scrubbing.

Concentrating on reaching Fairy, she stepped out the front door, before remembering that she wasn't sure if she could get back to Fairy. She walked to the backyard, through the border of blue spruce trees, and into a lovely green forest.

Fairy was still there.

The familiar path remained, with all the old landmarks still in place. The greens of the trees and grasses had deepened as spring had progressed. More flowers waved their cheery, colorful heads at her as she passed.

But in the meadow, a stark forbidding ruin contrasted sharply with the remembered comfort of a thin trail of smoke emerging from a tall chimney atop a proud, strong spire.

Hesitantly, Piper approached the ruins of the tower. The open doorway offered no hindrance to her admittance, so she peeked in, then walked in.

The roof was completely missing. The noonday sun bore down the well created by what remained of the stone walls. Piper could see through the missing stones to the meadow beyond. Weeds had grown up between and on top of the rocks that had once been a floor. The fireplace beneath the wreckage of the chimney looked forlorn and tragic without a roaring fire to dispel the upstart weeds attempting to pull it down.

No furniture of any kind remained. The interior stairs and upper floors must have been made of wood because the only sign of their previous existence was a discoloration on the stones in their likeness and positions. The only sign of life was a bird's nest, high up the wall in a hole made by the falling of a stone.

A series of giggles in a tinkling chord brought Piper out of the ravaged spire. Near the quaint, arched, wooden bridge, several fairies darted and flew about. Piper recognized them.

"Figwort! Meadowsweet! Horsemint! Bearberry! Pasqueflower! You're back. It's wonderful to see you again!" She hurried toward the bridge as the fairies flew toward her.

"Who is it?"

"She's human."

"Couldn't be."

"How's she know us?"

"If she's from the Human world, she couldn't know us."

"She called us by name, fool."

"Dimwit."

"Idiot!"

"Simple wings!"

The fairies flitted in circles and figure eights around Piper, occasionally diving at one another or Piper. Piper held out her hand palm down for one to land. As she expected Meadowsweet alighted daintly on her hand.

"I met you when I first came here with Aelvarim." Piper smiled, and with her other hand fingered the blue-rock talisman Malraux and Aelvarim had made for her, hanging on its chain, nestled under her shirt. She wondered if it would still work, if the magic was still in force since its creator no longer existed.

"Who's Aelvarim?"

Piper sighed. She'd hoped someone would remember Aelvarim, other than herself. "An elf. He brought me to Fairy to help him solve my great-grandmother's murder. Larkingtower the wizard lived in the spire and Malraux in the cave." Meadowsweet looked at her like she was insane. "You tried to tease Aelvarim, and when that didn't work, you started pestering me, so I gave you a lock of my hair to let me go."

A cunning look crept over Meadowsweet's face; she took a step forward on Piper's hand, and leaned close. "I don't remember any of that, but perhaps if you were to give me another lock of hair, I could compare it with what I already have, and then I'd remember."

"I don't think so," Piper said.

Meadowsweet flew up off of Piper's hand, enraged. Before the fairies could attack her, Piper pulled the blue rock out, and the fairies flew away, disappearing under the bridge.

Obviously the talisman still worked. Piper crossed the bridge, but the fairies didn't come out. She thought about the encounter as she walked along the path. Was it significant that Aelvarim's magic still worked even though he wasn't there? She wished she knew more about how magic worked.

Malraux's grove was still weed-choked, and nothing remained on the hill where Aelvarim's house had once stood.

The fairies either hadn't emerged yet when Piper returned, or else they had hidden themselves at the sound of her footsteps. She saw nothing of them.

Slumping into one of the hard kitchen chairs back at the house, Piper wished that someone other than she remembered Aelvarim. At least then she could be certain she wasn't crazy for recalling memories of him.

Harm. Africa and Sherlock. They'd all mentioned Aelvarim.

People from her world remembered him; denizens of Fairy had no recollection of him. So he had existed, and she wasn't crazy.

Well, maybe only a little crazy.

As Piper sat contemplating this, Grandma faded into the chair opposite her.

"Well, dear, how's it coming?"

"I've finished typing your manuscript. I'll print it after I finish editing it for spelling and grammar. There were some parts I had questions about. I wondered if you'd mind me making some small changes."

Grandma shook her head. "Not that story, this story.

I don't care what you do with that story. I want you to fix this one. It's more important."

"Oh. The fairies are back, but they don't remember Aelvarim, or Malraux, or Larkingtower. However, Africa and Sherlock remembered Aelvarim, as did Harm, one of the women at work." Piper ran one finger in circles on the tabletop. "But I don't know what any of that means or how I'm supposed to fix things."

"Don't be silly. If you think it through, you'll see it immediately," Grandma scolded. "Obviously I'm not supposed to be here and Aelvarim is. That's what you need to change."

"How?" Piper nearly shouted. "I don't know how."

"Have you tried any spells, dear?" Grandma asked.

"Spells? Which spells?"

"Whatever spells you know, of course."

"I don't know any. Except for locate. I don't think that would be of any help now."

"You must be able to do something; otherwise, you wouldn't have found that statue that Malraux carved. You wouldn't still have your talisman against the fairies." Grandma sighed in a most unghostly way. "Dear, do try something." She quickly faded away.

What do I have to lose? Piper mused quietly to herself. She relaxed in her seat and concentrated on how much she wanted to find Aelvarim. Her heart fairly leapt inside her, pounding out a heavy, quick beat. But nothing else happened.

She went to the bedroom and flopped on top of the soft covers on the bed to contemplate the faded floral underside of the canopy. That didn't work, so she decided to recheck the computer version of the manuscript for spelling errors. Toward the end, she started reading instead of just spell checking.

The heroine fell in love with the elf, and the story ended happily.

Remembering her reaction to the locate spell, Piper wondered if that meant Aelvarim was in her heart. Had she fallen in love with him? Were her feelings deeper than just profound lust?

Admitting to herself that she loved Aelvarim was easier than deciding if this new ending of the manuscript had anything to do with it. Was she being manipulated by the very words written by her great-grandmother words she herself had typed into the computer?

No. Piper had found Fairy enchanting from the beginning. While the sight of Aelvarim had produced normal, healthy levels of excitement, she had done more— or should she say less, perhaps differently—than she would with only lust as her motivation. If she'd only wanted his body, she could have found easier ways than trying to track down her great-grandmother's murderer. Say, kissing him in the kitchen.

If only she knew how to pull him from her heart and put him in the chair on the other side of the kitchen table.

Piper rechecked the last several pages of the manuscript file with the spell checker, certain that she'd missed several misspellings. She had. How would Grandma's plucky heroine have put things right?

She'd just ask the elf for help.

That wouldn't work. For one, Aelvarim, the elf, had disappeared and couldn't help Piper. Secondly, Aelvarim claimed he didn't know much of magic, just a few simple spells. He'd said he was a storysmith, and asked Piper's help to fix the story. Of course that could mean that Piper had power and abilities she knew nothing of.

Power and abilities she knew nothing of, a lot of good that did her. Realizing her logic was leading her in circles, Piper saved the file and shut down the computer. Too bad she couldn't just edit her life like she could Grandma's manuscript. Eliminate all the mistakes and false starts and wrong turns, and force everything to make sense. That would make so many things so much easier.

Staring at the computer, Piper wondered if it could really be that easy. Aelvarim had said that stories written in the Human world changed the world of Fairy.

Piper rebooted the computer. She didn't have a whole story, plot, characters, and all, but she did have an idea. Would that be enough?

She opened a new file, and typed, "And she found him sitting at the kitchen table waiting for her."

The chair across from her remained empty. Maybe it had to be printed on paper. Grandma had been able to make some small changes with a handwritten manuscript. Or had they been merely suggestions and clues?

The printer was still in her suitcase in the bedroom. Unfortunately, the kitchen hadn't been built for an excess of electrical appliances. Piper had been using the upper socket of the only outlet along the wall for the computer. She discovered the lower one didn't work by plugging first the printer, then the handheld mixer into the lower socket. The other outlets in the room were too far away for her printer cable to stretch. An outlet in the bedroom was situated such that she could connect the computer and the printer.

Piper sighed as she heard the printer in the bedroom finally whir to life, and begin printing her single, small sentence. She snatched the page up as it spewed, still warm and smelling of ink, from the printer, and read it with great satisfaction.

Walking into the kitchen with high hopes, Piper looked to the chairs at the kitchen table.

They were empty.

TWENTY ONE

"WELL IT WAS A GOOD TRY, DEAR," GRANDMA said. She hovered, translucent and pale, by the back door. "I really thought it would work."

Piper tried to hide her disappointment. "Why didn't it work? What did I do wrong?"

"I don't know, dear." Grandma floated over to the kitchen table and appeared to sit on one of the chairs. She became more opaque and solid-looking as she sat. "Did you concentrate hard enough? Put your whole heart and soul into it?"

Tears welled up in Piper's eyes. "I thought I did. I really wanted to have him back. I really miss him. I didn't think I would. Before all this I thought I just wanted to have a normal, ordinary, average life. Without the usual insanity that seems to accompany our family. Now I'd give anything to have an eccentric, strange, wonderful, fantastic life. To have him back."

Her tears streamed down her face, dropping onto the floor, her hands, and the newly printed paper. Piper tried to wipe her eyes, but since she used the hand with the paper in it, she only succeeded in getting the paper wetter.

The paper warped from the wetness, but the ink didn't smear. Oddly, all Piper could think was that she must have a good printer if its output could stand up to this.

She folded the paper. "Maybe the problem is that I just hope he'll return, but I haven't believed it."

"Sometimes hope is all you've got to work with, and usually that's enough," Grandma said.

Drying her eyes with a kitchen towel, Piper nodded. More to placate Grandma than anything else.

A crooked smile stole across Grandma's face. "What I remembered most about spells is that they seemed to be more wish fulfillment than actual power, except of course in Fairy, where magic is power. The strength of will and burning desire seemed to be the most important components of any spell."

"Wish fulfillment," Piper said. She looked at the folded paper in her hands. "I wish. Don't I just wish he'd walk in the back door now."

The back door remained closed.

Sighing, Piper walked to the back door and looked out. No one was there. She looked again at the wet, warped, folded paper in her hands. Would spindling or mutilating it help any? She held it in the rip in the wall where she'd found the first ending to Grandma's manuscript.

"I wish it were true, that Aelvarim was sitting in the chair and Grandma with Grandpa, and I wish it with all my heart." Piper dropped the paper into the hole.

It fluttered, scratching softly against the inner sides of the wall, and disappeared from sight.

Piper turned to look at Grandma. "Any ideas?"

"Not a one, dear."

Fix the story. How could she fix the story? Piper crossed the kitchen to sit on the hard chair across the table from her great-grandmother's ghost. Watching Grandma intensely for any reaction, Piper asked, "Do you think changing that story would fix this story?"

"What do you mean?"

"You said earlier that you wouldn't mind if I made changes in your story. Is it possible that changes in the story you wrote could change what's happened, fix things?"

"It's worth a try, dear." Grandma faded away.

Piper stared at her computer screen for a few minutes thinking. If she changed the story so that somewhat before the end the elf disappeared, then returned to help set things straight for the heroine, maybe that would be enough of a difference to fix the mess Piper had made. As she made the changes to the manuscript file, Piper thought about Aelvarim, and Fairy, and her own world.

She was real, and Aelvarim was from Fairy, but that didn't mean they couldn't love each other, want each other, grow together, be lifelong companions. Reality needed a dose of Fairy to be palatable and livable, and Fairy needed reality to exist at all.

It took until after sunset to finish making the changes she'd thought over. However, Aelvarim hadn't appeared. Unable to think of anything else she might do to the story that might change Aelvarim's and Grandma's situation, and worried that further changes might destroy a perfectly good story, Piper saved her work.

Almost automatically, Piper started printing out the story. Before the first page curled out, warm and crisp, from the printer Grandma appeared.

"All finished?" Grandma asked.

"I've done as much damage as I dare. You had a good story, I don't want to ruin it."

"I'm sure whatever you did was fine, dear." Grandma hovered over the printer for a while, waiting and watching each page as it came out of the printer. "What's wrong with this consarned machine? Why's it taking so long?"

Piper sat calmly in her chair. "The printer is fine. And it doesn't take any time compared with writing everything by hand."

Grandma floated back to the other chair. "You're right, dear. I'm just not as serenely patient as I used to be. I'm sure it'll work this time. I have a feeling."

"I don't know, Grandma." Piper stood up to go get the last pages from the printer. "I've already made all the changes to the story, and nothing happened. I'm just printing it so I have a hard copy, in case the computer crashes."

"It's all right," Grandma said, smiling at Piper. "Whatever happens, I want you to know that I love you, and I've always been pleased you were my great-granddaughter, and proud of who you are and what you are capable of."

"I love you, too," Piper called from where she crouched by the printer, waiting for the last page to curl out. "I just wish I could have done better for you." She picked up the last pages and carried them out to the kitchen. "Here we go," she said as she put them on the table and looked to the chair on the opposite side of the table.

Aelvarim sat in Grandma's seat at the kitchen table. Grandma was nowhere in sight.

He smiled at Piper. "I knew you'd rescue me. I knew you'd fix the story."

"What?" Piper demanded, surprised and pleased and scared.

He cringed. His smile slipped and became rather crooked and anxious. "Well, I hoped you'd rescue me. I hoped you'd forgive me for what happened here." He waved his hand around to indicate the kitchen, especially the counter. "My actions were quite improper and inexcusably base. I should not have made such unseemly advances toward you. I can only beg you now to forgive me."

"First," Piper shouted, advancing on him as he cringed and slunk down in the chair. My goodness but he was cute when he was nervous. His big blue eyes became even bigger, and his hair mussed itself up appealingly. "You haven't given me a chance to apologize for accusing you of murdering my great-grandmother. And I never, ever, intend to forgive you for making improper advances toward me. Never."

Piper plopped down to sit in his lap. Aelvarim's eyes widened in surprise, and hope.

"And you'd better never apologize for them either." She put her arms around him and kissed him.

It didn't take him long to catch up to her. He sat up and held her tightly in his warm, strong arms, and joined enthusiastically in the sweet lingering kiss.

"I missed you," Piper murmured into his ear when they came up for air sometime later.

"I'm here now. Forever."

"Good." She kissed him again, twining his silky dark hair through her fingers.

Much later as they walked through the dark backyard, past the old weatherworn gazebo to the majestic blue spruce trees, Aelvarim stooped to pick a small wildflower. He held it briefly under his nose, then smiled, before holding it out to Piper. "I wish I could compose sonnets to illustrate your wondrous qualities, expound your beauty, proclaim your intelligence, and extol your many virtues."

Taking the tiny, fragrant flower, Piper sniffed it while thinking. "Sonnets. You mean poems and such."

"Yes."

"Rhyming poems?"

"That is the accepted pattern, yes," Aelvarim said wryly.

Looking up through the trees, Piper caught a glimpse of the stars twinkling in the night sky. She turned her attention back to the path before she could trip on something. Aelvarim walked beside her, quietly; his feet didn't crunch in the leaves and pine needles coating the forest path. She glanced at him. "Would you have to rhyme my name?"

"Possibly." He looked daunted at the thought.

"Piper," she murmured. "Wiper, diaper, hyper." She shook her head. "No. I think I'd rather you didn't."

Aelvarim spread his hands. "There's always your last name."

"Pied." Piper frowned at him as she thought. "Hide. Wide. Tried. Lied. Cried. Fried. Died. Definitely not."

He chuckled. "There's always abide, or preside, or confide."

"Reside. Applied," Piper added.

"Side and all its variations."

"Piper Pied and cyanide! Formaldehyde! Insecticide!" Piper shouted.

"Perhaps not."

She grinned at him, glad to see that he, too, was smiling and not upset at her joking. "Definitely not. I don't think I'm the type to be immortalized in poetry. I'm not sure I want any of my actions in this last escapade recorded in story and song. I'd be afraid that generations from now someone would say, 'Let's hear it again. I love that part near the end when she makes all those stupid mistakes.'" When Aelvarim turned away to hide his smile, Piper added, "Someone else would be bound to say, 'Yeah. My favorite part is when she decides that the best way to get rid of the vines is to have the mage blast her with fire.'"

Aelvarim turned back, serious and staid. "Actually, I

was rather amazed at your ability to withstand such magic. Very few have such a high magical resistance."

"Don't tell me that's already someone's favorite part." Piper shuddered.

"No. Not at all. I merely found your tolerance level . . ." Aelvarim stopped, staring down the path.

Piper stopped, and looked in the same direction. A wispy curl of smoke rose from the dark chimney of a tall stone tower in the middle of the distant meadow to lazily cross the face of the moon. "Uh-oh. What are the chances that Larkingtower is back, too?"

"I don't know." Aelvarim reached for the harp at his hip. "Have you been in Fairy since the fight with Larkingtower?"

He listened intently as Piper explained what she'd found when she'd awoken in Fairy, and what she'd seen in her trips since. She told him about the statue, the empty ruined tower, the cavern, and the fairies.

"The statue, it only displayed the three of us, not Larkingtower?" When she nodded, Aelvarim drew a deep breath. "The only way we'll know for certain if Larkingtower is back is to knock at the tower's door."

The stone tower appeared much as it had in the days Larkingtower had lived there. It still seemed a massive spire of cold, forbidding stone, with few tightly shuttered windows, a solitary chimney, and a solid wooden door.

Hiding behind Aelvarim as he approached the reanimated structure to knock on the sturdy door was cowardly, but Piper couldn't help herself. It was all she could do to keep from clutching his cape and urging him to forget this and run. Aelvarim, however, walked resolutely to the door and rapped five times confidently.

Only the hand he kept on his harp betrayed his unease as the door slowly creaked open.

TWENTY TWO

"AELVARIM!" A SHORT, BALDING, ROTUND man exclaimed happily. He immediately began patting his robes as if looking for a pocket. "I've got it right here. I'm fairly certain. I thought it . . ."

The inside of the spire was almost too warm, a large fire blazed in an enormous fireplace. The floor was covered in a thick layer of papers, dirty dishes, expended candles, clothes, boots, and bits of junk. Shelves, lined with books and magical paraphernalia, clung haphazardly and crookedly to the walls. On the far side a wooden staircase leading to the upper floors huddled by the side of the wall, as if afraid to touch the mess. Two large, cushioned chairs sat by the fireplace like comfortable cats basking in the heat.

A change came over the expression on Aelvarim's face. He relaxed, and sighed. "Not to worry. I was just passing by and thought I'd save you the trip. I didn't mean to make more trouble for you."

"No trouble at all. No trouble at all." The man stroked his short graying beard, dislodging a few nuts from its tangles. He turned to search the room, patting along the mantel of the fireplace, upending cushions from comfy padded chairs, and tossing things onto the already-well-strewn floor. "I had it right—Ah-ha!" He held up a small, coverless, well-mended, dog-eared book. *Sonnets the Easy Way*. He noticed Piper for the first time and hid the book behind his back. "Oh, beg your pardon."

"You remember Piper," Aelvarim said.

"Yes." The man smiled a second. His smile slipped, then disappeared. He shook his head, jowls waggling. "That is, no."

"She lives in the house on the other side of the forest, at the juncture between Fairy and the Human world," Aelvarim patiently explained.

"Oh, yes." The man rubbed the side of his head, looked at Piper quizzically, and shook his head again. "I'll be forgetting my own name next."

"Which would be?" Piper asked.

"Ah . . ." He again began patting around for his pockets.

"Blendingstone," Aelvarim said firmly.

"Yes?" Blendingstone looked at Aelvarim as if expecting a question.

"We must leave now," Aelvarim said slowly and distinctly. "We need to find Malraux."

"Very good. Very good." Blendingstone waved good-bye with the book. "I'll just keep searching for that book for you, shall I?"

Taking the book from him, Aelvarim said, "No, thank you."

"Ah. I see you've got your own copy. Save me the trouble of finding mine."

Piper stepped in between them to ask Blendingstone, "Do you know Malraux?" At Blendingstone's confused look, she added, "Short fellow, leather apron, digs out rocks."

"Sounds like a dwarf," Blendingstone said. "Try looking in a mine, that's where you usually find them."

Aelvarim motioned for Piper to follow him out. "Thank you. Good night."

"Good night."

In the cool dark outside, Aelvarim smiled sheepishly as he tried to hide the book.

"Don't write any sonnets about me," Piper said.

"As you wish."

"So, how well do you know Blendingstone?" Piper asked as they crossed over the quaint wooden bridge.

"Fairly well," Aelvarim said. "You might not think so to see how absentminded he is, but he's a very good wizard."

"How long have you known him?" Piper asked.

"Years and years. He helped me enspell my house when I first settled here."

"And what about Larkingtower?"

Aelvarim stopped in his tracks, his mouth opening and closing. "I remember Larkingtower. He lived in the spire. But Blendingstone lives in the spire. Has for years. I . . . How very strange. I have two different memories for the last several years." He looked at Piper, his expression a mixture of shock and wonder. "I remember what happened. I remember what didn't happen. And they're both true. How very odd."

"And Malraux? Does he still live here?" she asked, very quietly.

"I don't know." Aelvarim thought about it for a moment. "I honestly don't know."

Piper grabbed Aelvarim's hand and began dragging him behind her. "Come on. Let's find out."

Once he started she let his hand go. After a moment, Aelvarim said, "I should walk you home after we find out if Malraux is all right."

"That would defeat my purpose in walking you

home," Piper said. "I'd just have to do it again."

"That wouldn't work."

"We'll have to think of something else."

The sound of a hammer and chisel on stone echoed down the path. Piper and Aelvarim looked at each other, grinning like idiots.

"Malraux!" they both shouted, as they raced down the path.

"Where have you two been?" Malraux shouted back at them as he stepped out of the grove by his cave and onto the path.